J.L. POWERS

UNDER WATER

J.L. POWERS

UNDER WATER

FIRST EDITION
10 9 8 7 6 5 4 3 2 1

Library of Congress Cataloging-in-Publication Data

Names: Powers, J. L. (Jessica Lynn), 1974- author.
Title: Under water / by J.L. Powers.
Description: First edition. | El Paso, Texas : Cinco Puntos Press, [2019] |

Sequel to: This thing called the future. | Summary: After her beloved grandmother's death, seventeen-year-old Khosi is left with an empty house, her younger sister, and her promise to finish school but violence in Imbali may take even that.

Identifiers: LCCN 2018027161| ISBN 978-1-947627-03-1 (cloth : alk. paper) | ISBN 978-1-947627-04-8 (pbk. : alk. paper) | ISBN 978-1-947627-05-5 (e-book)
Subjects: | CYAC: Coming of age—Fiction. | Healers—Fiction. | Sisters—Fiction. | Zulu (African people)—Fiction. | Blacks—South Africa—Fiction. | South Africa—Fiction.
Classification: LCC PZ7.P883443 Un 2019 | DDC [Fic]—dc23
LC record available at https://lccn.loc.gov/2018027161

Cover and book design by Antonio Castro H.
Cover photo by Izak de Vries. Capetown, South Africa.

For Dumisani Dube

brother and friend

1960-2017

CHAPTER ONE

THREE YEARS AGO

I don't know how or when the amadlozi choose someone—if you are destined from birth or if, at some point when you are growing, they notice something, they point to it, they say, There, there, right there, that one—she is meant for us. She will be our voice to the people.

Chosen.

Chosen means you don't choose. Somebody else chooses for you. In this case, all the people who come before you. Your ancestors. Your mothers, fathers, grandmothers and grandfathers, all the greats backing up for all of time to the beginning of earth. They will not give up until you answer. And your answer must be "yes" or you will go crazy.

Mina, I was chosen three years ago. Mama was dying of the disease of these days. A neighbor sent a witch to curse us. A man was stalking me. And through all of that, they came. They spoke. Hamba, they said. Hamba.

They spoke the same word over and over until I obeyed, until I started walking—not in any particular direction, just wherever they said to go. Here, there—a circuitous journey that finally led me right back to my home here in Imbali, the place of flowers.

They led me to the mountains. I scaled boulders, slipped on icy slopes, froze fingers. They led me deep inside a bowl of sandstone rock that looked as though only the Lord of the Skies could live there in its cold, barren beauty. I soaked in its silence until they led me out again.

They led me into the forest. I sat at the foot of a tree, for days, waiting. I didn't even know what I was waiting for. But then the trees spoke, not with human voices but something deeper that I felt through the earth and the trunk and the leaves. They told me which plants could heal bronchitis, which could give the sick an appetite, which could cure depression and loneliness. I gathered winter herbs, crushed and dried them, and stored them in bags that hung from the belt slung around my waist.

And then they led me to the river. The Thukela.

It was swollen with spring rains—the waters choppy, angry. I sat on the edge, knowing I could not cross. I do not know how to swim, and what about the crocodiles? This is what I told Mkhulu, the ancestor who first called me, the one who spoke to me more than any other. I imagined myself flailing around. Sucked under. Water filling my lungs. Choking me. Perhaps a crocodile grabbing me with its powerful teeth and making a meal of me.

Step into the water, Mkhulu said.

I sat very still in disbelief.

Go into the water, he said.

I will drown, I said.

You will not drown.

Tiny drops of water flicked up from the swirling rapids and rained down on me. A giant rapid swooshed directly toward me and drenched me. I retreated.

It was almost as if, the longer I sat there, the angrier the water grew. And then it was swelling and growing, overflowing its banks, little rivulets reaching me where I stood.

Go into the water, he said.

I wasn't prepared for this. I wasn't prepared that this might be the way I die. That after burying Mama, after leaving Gogo and Zi behind for this journey, that I might be saying goodbye forever. That my crazy, rabid ancestors were actually out to kill me.

A snorting, shuffling sound from behind. Hot breath on my ankles. A crocodile lumbering toward the water. Toward me. Dear God, hopefully it isn't hungry, I prayed. I hoped it wouldn't follow me into the water—because that was where I was going, even if I didn't want to.

The water was ice cold. Bumps sprang up all over my skin. The crocodile let loose a long, low growl.

I was in as deep as my waist, hesitating. You didn't have to send a crocodile to push me in, Mkhulu.

It opened its mouth, snapped its teeth.

Or maybe you did.

I wanted to believe I wasn't afraid of death. After all, I had seen my Mama cross the river and join the amadlozi on the other side—the ancestors, so numerous they were like a herd of black and white striped amadube crossing the plains. They welcomed her with joyous cries. My very bones were certain of this truth: that death is just the next thing after this thing.

But still…

Mkhulu, I said, as the crocodile nudged me deeper into the watery depths. I'm not ready to die.

CHAPTER TWO

Promise

My grandmother Gogo's voice is in my head even before Zi throws the first handful of dirt on her grave. *Don't forget your promise, Khosi. Don't forget.*

Dust chokes my throat as I turn away. A speck of dirt flies into my eye and I rub until it's raw. Tears drip down my cheeks. Even the woman keening or the call and response of the others in the crowd, mourning the loss of my grandmother, can't drown out her voice. The priest in his black robes stands in front of her grave, leading the people in prayer, and still, I hear *her* voice over the ancient words of the church, chanted by a hundred mourners.

You promised, Khosi. You promised. Don't forget.

It's true, before she died, I promised Gogo exactly two things. They seemed small at the time. If I'd known what it meant to make those promises, I would have kept my mouth shut. But I said yes. And now I can't back out. The dead have access to me twenty-four hours a day, seven days a week. They hound me with their commands. Do this. Do that. Go there. Fetch that. And Gogo's dead now. So I have no escape. She will harass me until I do what I said I would do.

I take my sister Zi's hand. She looks up at me, total trust reflected back in her eyes.

Zi's nine. I'm only seventeen but I'm all she has left—Mama dead for three years and Gogo three days now. Baba has never been involved in our lives, even less so after Mama passed.

OK, Gogo. I'll keep my promises. I'll keep them, even if it kills me.

CHAPTER THREE

ACCUSATION

We make a procession from the cemetery to the house, walking up and down Imbali's dirt roads. Winter is dry, the roads covered with a thick centimeter of reddish-brown earth. The morning haze has lifted, cold air gradually giving way to the heat of day.

Most of the neighborhood and all of my grandmother's family are here, dressed in their funeral best. Mama's sister's family walks in front of us, Auntie Phumzile dressed in her Zionist church service finery—a white turban wound around her head, white blouse and green skirt, a maroon cape wrapped around her shoulders. My cousin Beauty, too, is dressed in an expensive new dress, and she walks with her head held high. She barely acknowledged me when she arrived. My mother's brother is dressed in his finest suit and he carries Mkhulu's walking stick, my grandfather's staff that was passed down to the new patriarch of the Zulu clan when he died.

Zi and I are wearing simple, everyday clothes, like Gogo requested— white, her favorite color.

My neighbor MaDudu walks alongside us and clucks her tongue. "Didn't you and Zi buy new clothes for your grandmother's funeral?"

"We didn't have the money," I explain. "Anyway, Gogo chose these dresses for us to wear to her funeral. They were her favorites. She said she lived an ordinary life and she wanted her real life honored in that way."

I remember her smile as she told me, "You arrive Mr. Big Shot but leave Mr. Nobody. I don't need an expensive funeral, eh, Khosi?"

"Shame," MaDudu says, agreeing with my decision, and nods her chin at Auntie Phumzile. "But that one, she will say you aren't showing proper respect."

Of course MaDudu is right. Auntie will say these things, but she will be wrong. This is how I offer respect to Gogo—by following her wishes. And by keeping my promises to her, even though, only seventy-two hours after her death, it seems impossible.

We turn the corner to our street and I stop for a moment, just to look at the people coming to mourn Gogo.

In the past week, our yard was transformed so that we could host the neighborhood—a neighborhood Gogo has lived in for some forty years. We erected a large tent where neighbor women have been preparing the funeral meal. Already, the neighborhood is queuing, a line of people stretching from the gate to the spaza shop two doors down. The scent of fried chicken, rice, phuthu, and cooked kale hits my nose long before I reach the yard.

It feels like a betrayal to Gogo to be hungry but it's true, my stomach is growling. I need to eat now now. I have had just one or two slabs of phuthu with a little bit of amasi since she died, three days ago, a fact that Little Man has pointed out, worried that I'm going to collapse. "You need to eat, Khosi," he urged me. "To keep your strength up for all you must face."

But how could I eat, hearing all the rumors and accusations?

I grip Zi's hand even tighter. I can't forget Auntie's face, her lips curling, her nose twitching in sudden sneezes as she demanded the right to go through Gogo's things and take what she wanted. "I am her daughter, I should have her clothes," she claimed. "It is tradition."

As a sangoma, everybody believes that I revere and respect tradition more than anything else. But I must tell you, sometimes tradition cloaks thievery. Not that I cared about Gogo's clothes, but I would have liked to keep the simple beaded jewelry and headdress, just to remember her.

Instead, I have the house to remember her by, which presents a different problem.

For now, though, all I must think about is making it through the funeral.

Zi and I stop first at the washing station to clean our hands before we enter the house after having visited the gravesite. Inside, family members are already feasting. I scan the queue for Little Man and his parents. To me, and to Gogo, Little Man is family but I understand that nobody else recognizes that—yet—so he must stay outside with the others. Maybe someday the rest of my family will understand that even if we are only 17, we have been together for three years, ever since Mama's death. He is much more than a boyfriend.

Inside, there are no places for us to sit except the floor, so we take a corner and wait for one of the ladies to bring us plates of food. I suppose we better get used to sitting on the floor. Auntie also claimed the sofa in the living room and the table in the kitchen. I'm hoping my uncle will step in and tell her no. No, no, you cannot leave Khosi and Zi with nothing. This is their home too…that is what I hope he will say.

Auntie flounces over to the floral sofa she wants. She sits with a big plate of food balanced on her lap, glancing at me from time to time as she chews the meat off a bone.

"Mm mm, I'm just saying, why did my mother die so suddenly after she made a will and left the house to Khosi?" She is talking to Gogo's niece from the Free State, who drove all night to get here for the funeral.

"Sho, is it?" The niece bites into a hunk of meat.

I put my plate of food down on the floor, stomach churning. What's going to happen after all the food is eaten and the neighbors go home? What will Auntie say then? Or do?

"I'm sure Elizabeth's daughter would never harm a soul," the niece says. "I know Khosi is a sangoma but she doesn't practice this thing of witchcraft, does she?"

"I never thought so, not while Mama was alive." Juice drips down Auntie's wrists as she mixes gravy with phuthu and scoops it into her mouth. "But you never know with sangomas, not these days. It is very suspicious that my mother died so soon after she wrote that will."

"What what what, you really believe she is umthakathi?"

I can't listen to this. "Come, Zi," I say, and we stand and walk out of the house. As we pass, my aunt cackles under her breath, knowing she's scored a point against me.

I slink outside, an unwanted dog in my own house. The crowd of people waiting to eat is as long as ever and the yard is already festering with trash and flies. This is going to be some clean up job… I only hope my family members, the vultures who have descended for food and a chance to take all of Gogo's things, will stay long enough to help me clean up.

I wait in the yard, saying goodbye to neighbors and friends as they leave. "Hamba kahle," I tell yet another neighbor, who looks satisfied by his big meal.

"Sala kahle," he responds.

The priest who spoke at the funeral takes my hands gently in his. Droplets of sweat glisten in his short, wiry hair. He must be sweltering in those dark priest's robes.

"Baba," I greet him.

The fact that I am a sangoma lays between us, unspoken. I have never felt that I couldn't be both Catholic and a sangoma, I have never felt there was a contest between God and the amadlozi, but I am not sure that he—or other priests—feel the same way. And it is true that God is silent and the amadlozi speak to me all the time. Why would God choose to be quiet when I know he could speak? So perhaps there is some contest after all. I am not sure what to do with this split in my heart.

"Khosi," he says. He lifts a hand and lays it on Zi's head. "I trust that we will see you and Zi at mass on Sunday, like always. That you will be as faithful as your grandmother was all her life."

"Yes, Baba." I skirt his eyes to look at the sky.

Zi gives him a hug. He makes a rumbling noise in his throat, a little sound of love and affection, and perhaps some sorrow too.

"I'll be praying for you," he says.

"Hamba kahle," I say, in return. I'm glad for his prayers. We need them more than ever.

After everyone is gone, Auntie sends her husband to borrow a friend's bakkie so they can take Gogo's sofa with them now now.

"It's OK, Auntie Phumzi," I say. "It is late. Come back tomorrow. The sofa will still be here. It is not going to disappear overnight."

She laughs. "Oh, no, by then you will bewitch it. I must take it now, before you do something evil like you did to my mama."

"I would never hurt Gogo," I say. I look from Auntie to my cousin Beauty and then to my uncle Lungile. "Beauty?" My cousin and I have always been different, in many ways, but she and I are close in age and played together growing up. I would like to think she is an ally. "Uncle?"

The awkward moment stretches out like a pot of phuthu and amasi that must feed too many mouths.

"Let us just focus on the future," Uncle says finally. He scratches his head, as though trying to distract us from what he is saying. "Let us leave this thing behind us."

"What thing?" I ask. "This thing of Auntie accusing me of something I would never do? Do you really think I would hurt Gogo? Gogo, the only mother I had after my own mama died?"

"Nooooo," Uncle says. "But you must listen to your auntie."

It is nonsense, what he is saying. If I did not kill Gogo through witchcraft, but that is what she is saying, why must I listen to her? I can see I have lost my family through this.

"Take what you want." I am angry now. It burbles up in my chest, the same anger I once felt towards Mama when I realized she stole money before she died. "I do not care about things. I have Gogo's spirit with me, which is more than you will ever have. And I have the house, you cannot take that."

Somehow those words take Auntie from one thing to another, and in seconds, she is screaming. "We'll get the house back, you little witch," she yells. "You don't deserve it! You killed her!"

"Phumzile!" Uncle Lungile shouts. "Quiet! You can't say these things, Mama is just now buried… Please, let this thing rest."

"Auntie," I say, pleading with her. I try to catch her eye but she refuses to look at me. "We are family. We are blood. Please, let us just let this thing go away."

But she won't stop. She's in my face, shouting. "It will never go away!"

Suddenly, I'm no longer afraid. None of the others can see Mkhulu or Gogo in the corner, but I can. They are shaking their heads—at her behavior, yes, but also at me, warning me to let this go, not to retaliate. So it's true, I'm not afraid. But my calm seems to convince her more than ever that I am guilty. I reach out to touch her forearm, to soothe her.

She jerks her arm away and raises her hand to slap me. "Hheyi, wena, you think we don't know what you have done? Hah!"

My cheek tingles from her slap. But the hurt feels good. Not like this thing of Gogo's death, a sting that will never go away.

"What is it you think I have done?" I say.

She spits in my face. "You killed her! You killed her!"

Uncle Lungile grabs her by the arm and hauls her outside. She's still shouting, and all the neighbors are gathering to watch. "Haibo! Go away or we will give you something to talk about," Auntie yells at them.

They move further up the hill but none of them stop watching. It is too good, this scene of family disarray. Even MaDudu stands and watches this thing of my aunt accusing me of witchcraft.

There are people who think it is powerful for others to believe you have a witch working for you, and I know there are those people who will seek my services if they believe that is what I do. But it is dangerous. It is not some game to play.

A long time ago, around the time Mama got sick with the disease of these days, MaDudu employed a witch to curse our family. She did it because she was angry. To our shame, my mama had stolen the insurance money after MaDudu's husband died, something we did not discover until after Mama died and I found the money she had hidden in a secret bank account. It has sometimes made me wonder if Mama can even be an ancestor, the way my Gogo and Mkhulu are. Yes, I watched her join the rest of the amadlozi when she died, and I often see her in the crowd that follows me around, but she never speaks to me. I never ask her for help to heal. I wonder if she even can help? Do the things we did or failed to do on earth prevent us from being fully what we should be on the other side too? I wish I knew. It's something I'm working out.

Auntie and Uncle stand a long time in the yard talking. Uncle holds her by the arm as if trying to prevent her from running away. She is talking so angrily, she doesn't even notice that her turban has come askew.

Her husband arrives in a borrowed bakkie and Uncle Lungile comes inside and says, "Khosi, the house is yours but you must leave just now. She will not come inside if you are here but it is our tradition for her to take her mother's things."

So Zi and I stand in the back yard, near the washing bins where we wash our clothes, while Auntie and her husband haul away the sofa and the table and chairs. They pack away most of the kitchen items, but leave us some few plates and forks and a pot for cooking. They leave us the beds and mattresses, for which I am grateful. And the TV. Perhaps they leave the TV because it is old. Their TVs are all new and this one wouldn't even fetch a good price if you tried to sell it in the streets.

And then they leave, all of them, they do not even come to the back to say goodbye or tell us they are done.

I wonder if they will be back for more or if we have seen the last of them.

CHAPTER FOUR

Lucky

When they are gone, Zi and I clean the mess. The women did dishes and packed up the remaining food—at least Zi and I have plenty to eat for the next week—but they left big piles of rubbish in the yard, which are already attracting flies. Zi and I pile the rubbish into several bins and cover them with a tarp. I can handle snakes or fleas or monkeys, even flies I can live with, but I hate rats.

"What do you suppose Gogo is doing right now on the other side?" Zi asks.

I shake my head. I don't have to suppose. I already know. "She and the other amadlozi are sitting around gossiping about the funeral," I say. "Gogo is laughing about how many people came for a free meal, people who never visited when she was alive."

Zi shakes her head. "That isn't funny," she announces. "I'd be angry. What good is it to come pay your respects after somebody dies if you never visited when they were here with us?"

"The things that matter to us when we are alive are not so important when we are dead," I say. "Gogo is glad they had a good meal. And she's touched by how many of them brought money to give to us."

Neighbors and friends, far and wide, gave what they could. 10 rand here, 50 rand there—it adds up. Most of it already disappeared to pay for the funeral expenses. What is left, Auntie and Uncle took a share of and left some few rands for me and Zi. They must feel they couldn't leave us with nothing, and yes, they were her children so they deserved something, probably the lion's share, which in fact they took. But it showed us, Zi and I are now on our own. We won't see any help from them for school fees or any other such needs.

"But don't you think Gogo is sad not to be here anymore?"

"She doesn't even miss us," I say. "She sees us anytime she wants. So if you ever want to talk to her, just say, 'Sawubona, Gogo!' Even if you can't hear her, she'll hear you!"

The look on Zi's face is one of pure horror. "No thank you," she says. "Does she really see everything?"

I suppose that is a scary thought for those who do things they shouldn't do. But I'm used to it.

The gate rattles and jangles. Little Man's outside, shaking the fence to be let in. I send Zi out with the key to unlock the gate while I haul a mattress from the bedroom to the living room so we have something to sit on.

I look up and Little Man catches me in a hug. He's like a Cape Holly or a lavender tree, he's grown so tall—tall but very thin, while I am short with lots of curves. I like the way it feels as his hand slips around my waist. And I still love his dark blue-black skin, just as much as when I first noticed it three years ago. "S'thandwa, how are you?" he asks.

I sink into him. This man. "Ngikhathele. How are you?" I ask. Instantly, I feel better as I hear his heart beating against my ear. He drapes his hand around my shoulder, his face close to mine, cheek to cheek. Perhaps I am not so tired as I seemed.

"I was just that much sorry not to be able to help more with the funeral," he says. He looks around the room. "Eish, it's empty. Relatives stole your furniture, eh?"

"They are angry," I say. "They think I killed Gogo."

He shakes his head. "Wena, you killed Gogo? They've gone mad, Khosi. How could they even think such a thing?"

"I don't know what to do," I admit. I know it makes you sad, Gogo, but I think they will have very little to do with me or Zi after this thing. I am sorry, I wish I knew how to heal this rift.

"Where's Zi?" I ask.

"She's outside with a little surprise." Little Man bursts out laughing. I've always loved his laugh. It booms out, like it's coming from a place deeper inside him than words. "Something I've brought for you."

"What?" I ask. Then, when he doesn't answer, "What what what?"

And then Zi is there opening the door and giggling and then she's running out into the yard with a little brown yapping thing biting her ankles and barking.

"What is this thing?" I ask. "A puppy? Why are you bringing me a puppy?" Gogo! You never let us have a dog and here you are, some three days gone, and I'm already breaking one of your rules. At least, this is not a rule you made me promise to keep.

Little Man has a sudden pleading look in his eyes. I already know what that look means, the content of his unspoken question.

When Gogo got sick, and we knew what was coming, it was something the two of us talked about, dreamed about. Being a family. Being together, all the time, living together. But Gogo made me promise to finish school before Little Man and I became serious.

But Gogo, how can you wait to get serious about somebody? Either you are or you aren't. And we always have been serious about each other, from three years ago, from the first time we kissed.

Plus, we never talked about what I should do if I was unable to finish school. What if I can't pay the school fees. What then? Am I never allowed to get serious about Little Man? Eh, Gogo?

"You know the answer is no," I say. "You cannot live with us. Not yet." I watch Zi, running after the little brown dog. She looks back at me, delight in her eyes.

"Eish, Khosi, do you think that's all I think about?" he asks, but a small part of the light inside his eyes dies. "I know we must wait until after the cleansing, at the earliest. But could you promise to think about it?"

I keep my eyes on the puppy and Zi, not wanting to focus on his pain. I want it too. Mkhulu, can you talk to my Gogo and ask her why she made me promise this thing? "Ehhe," I say. "Of course I will think about it."

The ritual cleansing after a loved one dies takes place some few weeks or months after their funeral. During that time, there are some few things you should not do, like drink alcohol, or you will not be able to stop doing that thing. Even if you don't want to do that thing, you will just keep doing it. You have no reason left, you are just an animal, doing what you do. So the cleansing has bought me some time to shield myself from Little Man's request.

"Anyway, that's why I'm giving you this dog," Little Man says. "You and Zi are too much alone. She will protect you. And did you know this dog chose us?"

"Eh? Is it?" I kneel down and call the puppy over with my tongue, tch tch tch tch. She joggles over and sits in front of me, tongue protruding, head tilted to examine us. She licks my hand as I look her over. She's nondescript, clearly a mutt, brown hair with black markings around the paws. She looks like she will grow up to be fat, one of those dogs that lays in the sunshine and barks ferociously at whoever walks past but then, if someone actually comes in the door, she'll waddle over to lick their hand. "Why do you say she chose us?"

"I was driving to Maqongqo to visit Baba yesterday," he says. "I was sad, thinking about your grandmother's death, and the funeral today. I didn't have my mind on driving. You know that part in the road when there's nothing but bush surrounding you as far as the eye can see? One of those bends in the road when you know you're kilometers away from where anybody lives—and you think maybe just now a lion will jump out in front of the car?"

"Yebo," I say. I love roads out in the middle of nowhere like that. It makes life seem wide-open with possibilities—not the closed-off feeling I sometimes get here in Imbali, with so many houses and people, you can't even see past your neighbor's house.

"Well, it was just then that I realized I had a flat."

"Haibo! Did you have a spare?"

"That's why I stopped. I got out to change my tire. And there she was, on the side of the road, poking her head out from the bush."

"Shame! How did she get way out there?" I ask.

"Who knows? Maybe somebody abandoned her. Or she walked there, but it must have been 50 K to the nearest house. Let me ask you, why did my car stop just then? At that exact spot? I will tell you why. Because she was waiting for me. For us."

We look at each other and then we look at the dog. And this is the thing: she looks guilty, like we've caught her out or something. Like she has chosen us, as Little Man says, but we weren't supposed to figure that out.

Gogo, I know you didn't like dogs. You said they were dirty creatures and belonged in the wild, on the savannas, not in our homes. Dogs and Zulus, you said, do not belong in the same hut. But I always felt vulnerable the way we lived, an elderly woman alone with two young girls. And now you're gone. What am I supposed to do? I need protection.

I know that tsotsis could just shoot a dog and come inside two seconds later and we'd have to face them. But I hate most the idea that I will have no warning, that death will be a surprise. I'd rather know I'm in danger than never see it coming.

"Will you take her?" Little Man says. "And it will make me feel you are safer, until the day when you say yes, and I can live with you."

Zi comes over and stands by the puppy. She tangles her fingers in the puppy's fur, looks at me with dark pleading eyes. How can I say no?

"Her name is Nhlanhla," I say. Lucky. She is lucky after all. Just because Little Man came along the road that day, she escaped certain death in the bush. She would have starved or been eaten by something bigger than her.

"Zi, don't just stand there," I say. "Go get her something to eat."

So her first night with us, Nhlanhla feasts on funeral food. "Don't get used to it," I tell her. "This is not how we normally eat."

She seems so smart, and her brown eyes—they look just like yours, Gogo.

"It's time for soapies," Zi says, hopeful.

So we turn the TV on. The three of us sit on the mattress, backs against the wall, the light flickering as we watch *Generations*, *Isidingo*, and *The Bold and the Beautiful*. Nhlanhla cavorts around the living room as Little Man reaches behind Zi's back to hold my hand, and I sit there with his hand in mine, feeling not quite so alone.

CHAPTER FIVE

The Cleansing

The empty house feels even more barren, stripped of most of the furniture and all the wall decorations and the crocheted lace that Gogo draped in various spots around the house. I hope Auntie is enjoying everything she took in her already over-decorated house.

When I think enough time has passed and I still haven't heard from them—not about the cleansing, not about life, not about school fees or help with what what, nothing—I visit my teacher, Makhosi. We must talk about launching my healing practice, especially if I must begin to earn a living.

Outside of the hut, her granddaughter Thandi stands in front of the washtub, plunging her arms deep into the sudsy water, apparently washing a load of clothing. She drips water on my shirt as she gives me a quick hug.

Thandi's little girl Hopeful is running in circles in the courtyard just inside their yard. Her mouth is sticky, stained red with some kind of candy.

"Are you coming to see me or is this a professional visit?"

"I'm sorry, I came to see your grandmother." I smile ruefully at her.

Thandi used to be my best friend. She and I have known each other almost our entire lives. But then she fell in love with an older man, Honest, who was anything but honest.

In truth, I haven't been the best friend to Thandi since Hopeful was born. First, I was training with her grandmother and going to school at the same time. Then Gogo got sick and died and now, it's just me and Zi, so I don't see how it's going to be different—I'm going to be responsible for a whole lot more now that Gogo isn't the adult. All this time, I've been trying hard just to manage everything. Besides, Thandi's entire life is so different than mine now. She quit school long before I did to take care of her baby. She and Honest stayed together for a short while but then he returned to his wife so she came back home. And now she's raising Hopeful alone, with her family's help, of course. It sometimes feels like we're both hiking a steep trail but the path is taking us up two completely different mountains.

"I'll tell Gogo you're here," she says.

"Ngiyabonga."

"Maybe after you can stay for a cup of tea and play with Hopeful?"

"Yebo." I nod my agreement.

Makhosi taught me everything I know. She trained me to be a sangoma. When she gestures, I enter her hut and breathe in the rich scent of impepho.

"Makhosi." I greet her with the honorific title.

"Makhosi." Before I became a full sangoma, when I was her junior, her student, she called me thwasa. Now she greets me as makhosi, her equal. Sometimes, now that people greet me the way they greet all sangomas, with a strong "Makhosi!," it feels as though my given name "Nomkhosi" with the nickname "Khosi" was nothing more than a prediction of my calling, of what I'd become someday.

I wait a few seconds in silence, out of respect. I expect her to ask me what I've come to ask her. But before I can talk to her about launching my practice, she reminds me that it's time to do the cleansing for Gogo.

"It's your duty," she says. "You must perform ukugeza. Then you can start your life. Your grandmother is waiting for this to be done. I can see her, can't you see her? She is crouching behind you, ashamed that her children have forgotten."

"I haven't forgotten," I say. "But I haven't heard from my aunt and uncle in three weeks. What if they don't want to do it? Or don't want to do it with me?"

"You do it on your own," she says, simply.

So I try calling Auntie and Uncle but neither answers the phone, nor do they call back. I text—*We need to do ukugeza, I am planning to do it, are you both coming?*—and hear only silence in return.

But you can't wait forever to cleanse the hut. At some point, life must return to the living. Even sangomas know this, we who are always with one foot in that world and one in this.

What should I do?

Go to her, my child, Mkhulu says. Your Gogo is here with us but she must have peace. Your Auntie Phumzile has forgotten tradition.

But what Mkhulu doesn't say, is this thing of accusing a relative of witchcraft—that is also tradition. Not real tradition. Not like a wedding or a funeral, where you can say, This is how things are done, nee? You have the food so, and the people so, and the impepho so, and here is where the amadlozi sit, and you must, you must, you must. But even so, these accusations, they happen all the time. What do you think of that, Mkhulu? Is that tradition, hah? Sometimes I am not so sure about "tradition."

Thandi and I have a quick cup of tea after but Hopeful is misbehaving, chasing after the dog and knocking into one of her grandmother's customers waiting in line, an elderly gentleman sitting on a broken chair. He wobbles for a second and then totters over, so slow it's almost comical.

"Oh, Mkhulu," I say, "let me help you up." He grips my offered hand and I raise him to standing position.

While I'm helping the old man, Thandi is already yelling at Hopeful and chasing her through the yard and into the house to swat her bottom.

I wait some few minutes, then tell Thandi I'll come by again soon. I'm so glad I'm not a mother yet.

That Saturday, Zi and I walk to the other side of Imbali to Auntie's house. They are home, I know this because her husband's car is there, and Auntie doesn't drive, but we rattle and rattle the gate and nobody comes out. We wait and wait. The sun beats down on us. We rattle again and wait. The dust rises and settles. Zi coughs. It feels like the grit is stuck in my throat.

"Why is Auntie rejecting us?" Zi asks. "Mama was her sister."

It does not make me proud to admit it, but I collapse at Auntie Phumzi's gate, sitting right there in the dirt as though I was a chicken or goat.

"What are you doing, Khosi?" Zi's voice rises high and shaky.

It's been three weeks since you left us, Gogo, and we're all alone. That is what I say to her.

But even as I wail silently, I know we're not alone. I have this cast of characters, as my drama teacher used to say, and they follow me everywhere, commenting on everything. Just now, they stare at me in stark disapproval. Get up, stop being a child, their stares say, even while their mouths remain closed.

"I don't know what to do, Zi," I say. "My spirit isn't in this fight. I just want to do what is right for Gogo. And for us, for the family. We must do the cleansing."

Zi rattles the gate and starts to call, "Auntie! Auntie Phumzi! You must come out. We must talk to you."

You're letting Zi do this alone, shame, Mkhulu says finally. You mustn't give up. Her voice is small and it doesn't carry, it's like a mosquito in a large room. Your voice will travel. You must just fly near your Auntie's ear so she cannot ignore you.

You cannot give up, my girl.

That is a new voice. A woman speaking. I peer at the people surrounding Mkhulu. Who is it, speaking to me? Who is this person? I have never heard her before. They gaze back at me, unperturbed. Any one of them can speak to me, and they are multitudes. But mostly, they let Gogo or Mkhulu speak.

"What are you looking at, Khosi?" Zi has turned back from the gate, defeated.

"Oh, nothing."

You mustn't be like the beasts of the field, those who graze and do not even know what they are eating.

It is that same voice again.

I'm not a beast of the field, I grumble at her, whoever she is.

"What, Khosi?" Zi asks.

Did I say that out loud?

"Please, can we go home now?" she asks.

That forces me to my feet. I stand and dust the dirt from my skirt. I do not have a loud voice either. Zi and I, we are just Imbali girls, trained to be quiet. But like Mkhulu says, I can send my voice right into Auntie's ear.

"Auntie," I say, as though she were standing right beside us. I picture my voice flying through the air, perching on her shoulder, speaking directly into her ear. "Auntie. We are here, and we are not going home until you come out and talk to us. If we start to yell, and make a scene, your neighbors will all come out and hear how you are neglecting your sister's children, how you are not willing to do ukugeza for your own mother. All the amadlozi are here with me, and if you think they won't help me, you are mistaken. I am the one they chose, I am a sangoma. I can hear them just as well as you can hear me now, even though I am nowhere near you."

"I'm here," Auntie says suddenly.

She stands by the gate, hair wrapped in a black turban. She's glaring at me so hard, her eyes bulge right out of her head. I want to tell her to stop staring or a bird will think her eyes are a ledge that they can land on. But I stay silent. Her husband and my cousin Beauty stand on the porch, keeping their distance.

"Speak, wena, and let us be done with it."

"We must do this thing," I say. "It's time."

"How can you do ukugeza?" Auntie protests. "You are not even wearing proper mourning clothes, hah! Are you going to burn your everyday clothes? And tell me, how will we buy a goat? Do you have so many rands that you can just go and buy one? If so, why are you not making your entire family rich, eh?"

I can't afford a goat, it's true, but it's also true that I know people, namely, a whole host of amadlozi, and they are on my side. They will help me. Auntie is forgetting that.

"I will get a goat," I say. "But you must come."

"How will you get a goat?" she shouts. "You see, hah! You can just conjure up a goat, like that. You are a witch. We will never come to your house. We will do our own ceremony here."

"Gogo is not here," I say. "She doesn't sit by your hearth in your hut. She is in my hut, at my hearth, in her own home. How can you do the cleansing here?"

But she is already gone, slamming the door behind her.

Zi and I are silent for a long time as we walk home. "How are we going to get a goat?" Zi asks finally.

I wish I knew. "You will see," I say.

How am I going to get a goat? It is not like goats wander the streets of Imbali, looking to be slaughtered so that you can do a cleansing for a loved one. Even if we were in the rural areas, goats are valued creatures.

Zi is asleep, taking a Saturday afternoon nap. It is a hot day and she grew sleepy. I would love to crawl in beside her and join her but I am vexed with this problem. We need to do the cleansing, and if I am on my own to do it, I am on my own.

Why can't it be a chicken, Gogo? A chicken I can find. A chicken I can buy, somehow. I can search for rands in the dirt, like a chicken pecking for food, and I can stand out on the street corners offering my services as a sangoma until enough people employ me so that I can buy a chicken.

I will tell you how to get a goat, my girl.

It is the voice of the woman again, the one who has never helped me before.

Go to the hill of the witch, she says.

I almost swear, I'm so startled. Words have power, so I keep a watch on my lips. But the witch? How could she suggest it?

I avoid the witch's hill scrupulously since that time, three years ago, when I encountered her. She had marked me, she was waiting for the chance to drag me underground where she planned to suck me dry of my life, my powers. She wanted to turn me into her own personal zombie, a slave that worked just for her. Little Man was the one to rescue me from her strong grip. And though I know I have the ancestors' protection now, and I think she will leave me alone, I am still afraid.

Even taxis avoid driving up that hill and past her house. Everyone knows she's a witch…everyone knows that young men and young women have disappeared, that she has turned them into zombies, that they go deep into the earth to find gold for her…and everyone's that scared of her. Just thinking about her makes me shiver.

Go to the witch's house, the woman says. You will find your goat tied to her tree in the front, outside of the gate.

Who are you? I ask.

I was trained to trust the amadlozi, without question. But this advice makes me very afraid. If the witch helps me, am I indebted to her? Am I allies with her, an evil one?

But you must do what they tell you to do. If my ancestor tells me to go to the witch's house, I must go. Otherwise, I will go crazy.

Who are you? I ask again.

She smiles at me and I realize she is one of my grandmothers, truly an ancient one, from long long ago.

Take a jar of amanzi, she says. Some of the ocean water you have blessed. It is powerful muthi. Leave it as payment for the goat.

Mkhulu, do you hear what this woman is saying?

Ehhe, he agrees but says nothing more.

But why would she help me? I argue. Because I cannot believe they are sending me to the witch, the one who tried to destroy me so long ago, before I realized I was meant to be a sangoma.

She will help because I compel her to help, the woman who is one of my grandmothers says. She has sins she must pay for.

So I go.

I thought I would avoid this side of Imbali the rest of my life. I know I am safe, at least with the amadlozi on my side, but it seems prudent to avoid your sworn enemy. Yet here I am, staggering up the hill.

It is very still up here, as if the wind itself refuses to breathe. Or as if the air is weighted with the heaviness of all the evil practiced in this place.

And it is just as my ancestor said. There is the goat, tied to the tree. The witch is nowhere in sight. I do not have to go to her house or speak to her, I can simply snatch the goat and leave.

I breathe a quiet sigh of thankfulness. That woman, eish, she truly does have sins she must pay for.

I leave the jar of amanzi—water I harvested from the Indian Ocean and then blessed with the words of the amadlozi—and I take the goat home. In the morning, I will ask Little Man to help me slaughter the goat. I will take the goat to emsamo, the place where the amadlozi sit in my healer's hut. I will burn impepho and speak to them. Zi and I will mix its stomach guts with water and wash outside. We will burn our mourning clothes, such as they are, since Gogo told us to wear our everyday clothes. And then, the cleansing will be complete.

As for me, I will be happy to have completed this important part of releasing Gogo to that side. But otherwise, I am uneasy.

I pray that the witch uses my amanzi for good, not evil.

I pray that I have not entered an unholy alliance.

CHAPTER SIX

Breaking Promises

Now that Gogo is gone, the days feel endless. It isn't that I am doing more work than before. In fact, I am doing less because I no longer need to care for her like I did while she was dying. But Gogo was always so joyful, even when she scolded and even when she was so sick she could barely breathe. Now her love is gone. That's not true, it is not gone exactly, it is just changed. Now she is one of the ancestors and it is no longer give and take. Her spirit is right here in the kitchen corner and her voice is in my head, talking, talking, talking. Khosi, do this. Khosi, do that. I am just a tool in her hands.

In fact, she is glaring at me.

What else could I do, Gogo? I ask.

Gogo hasn't been dead for a month and just today, I broke one of the promises I made to her—that no matter what, I'd finish school. I'd matriculate and then go to university.

You promised, Khosi. You promised you would finish school.

Yebo, impela, I promised, Gogo. I did. I know it.

I stare at the twenty rand note on the counter. It is all I have left after paying Zi's school fees this afternoon. There wasn't enough money for my fees also. And I have no one to go to for help. It's just me and Zi. Completely on our own. I have become what they moan about on the evening news: "a child-headed household."

I told all my teachers I'd return, soon, but I'm not sure any of us believe it. And it's the worst possible time for a student like me to quit—right in the middle of my matric year. The final year before university. I can't suddenly go somewhere else, like one of the fee-free township schools. They don't offer the same courses I've been taking. Even if they let me attend for the final half of my matric year, they've been preparing students for an entirely different set of exams than the ones I've been preparing for these past three years. Instead of being tested in Afrikaans or calculus, both classes I've been taking in preparation, they might test me in history and accounting.

For a long time now, my dream has been to go to school and be a nurse while also practicing as a healer. I was initiated as a sangoma just before Gogo caught pneumonia. The goal was to make some money as a sangoma while finishing school, to help pay my fees, but we all hoped I would get a bursary too. That was before, when we still had Gogo's pension from the government, and Uncle and Auntie were giving her some money each month to help raise us. Now, Zi and I are completely dependent on the money I make as a sangoma, for living as well as for school fees.

And it's not enough. At least, not yet. After all, I'm new. I still have to establish myself, create what my business teacher called "a customer base." It could have been more difficult if my teacher had asked me to go somewhere else to practice since she is already practicing here in Imbali. But Makhosi said there was more than enough for both of us and she will send me her overflow. I am grateful that she loves me that much, that I'm not just somebody she trained. I am truly her daughter.

Even so, there hasn't been much overflow. I need more customers if Zi and I are going to eat next month. But Gogo still expects that I would be able to pay for my school fees too?

I know I promised, Gogo, but that's before I knew how hard it would be. Would you have made me promise if you knew? I'd like to think you'd release me from an impossible promise.

But the dead broker no compromise. Right is right. The eye crosses the full river, Khosi, she used to say.

In other words, if I wanted it, I would make it happen, no matter how hard or seemingly impossible.

But Gogo, I do want it. I want to finish school more than anything. How am I supposed to go to school if I don't have the money to pay for it, eh, Gogo?

Sometimes when I talk to her about these things, the conversation is a one-way street. All she does is glare at me from wherever she is sitting or standing.

But now she speaks.

Don't tell me what what. You're a sangoma, my child, she says. You have a way to make money. Enough money to pay for school.

Perhaps in time, yes, but not so soon. That's what I want to say but I leave the thoughts in the part of my head she can't hear. It feels too disrespectful.

Plus, and this is not something I say to her, her daughter's accusations—my auntie's anger—may have made the neighbors afraid to visit me, to consult me as a sangoma.

But now that I'm not in school, I'll certainly have enough time to work. I don't say that to Gogo either.

And I don't say anything to Little Man when he comes over later that night. Perhaps because he has such excitement spilling from his eyes. He rattles the gate, sending Nhlanhla into a tizzy. She gallops toward him, goofy and long-eared, while I hurry out, fumbling with the lock. He picks me up, swings me around, grunts *oof*, and kisses me hard on the mouth. It leaves me breathless, he keeps his lips planted on mine so long. I take his hand and pull him inside. Zi is with my neighbor so if he's going to kiss me like that, he can do it without God and everybody watching, the sun shining on us with a bright intensity, almost as though scrutinizing our kisses.

As soon as the door shuts behind us, leaving Nhlanhla outside, shivering with whimpers, he reaches for me again.

I lean with my back against the wall and let him kiss me. Little Man has always liked to kiss me though usually they were stolen good-bye kisses, between the house and the gate when we were sure Gogo wasn't watching. Now he plants a series of quick, sweet ones on my lips, taking little breaths in between, and then a few long ones that make my knees shake. I grab his jacket to hold steady.

"I have a job," he announces.

"What?" I stare at him. This was not the plan. I'd take a step away but my back is literally against the wall. "I thought you had a bursary. That you were going to school."

"Eish, Khosi, I'm tired of school," he says. "I need a break."

It used to be when I stared at him, we were eye to eye. It made me feel more like equals. Now I have to look up up up at him, an elephant looking up to a giraffe.

"You never said that before," I say. "You were always studying. You liked science and math. You were—"

"I needed to pass matric," he interrupts. "It would be shameful to fail. But now, I'm going to work. So I can help you and Zi." And he leans in to kiss me again. His fingers graze my hips, his hand a firm grip on my back.

A little ball of anger mixed with happiness forms at the pit of my stomach. I am not sure which emotion is stronger. Of course I want—need—help. But I don't want him to quit school for me. "No," I say.

"Listen, Khosi," he starts speaking fast. "I know what you'll say but we have been together always, since we were young, and if I am making money, I can help you, so you can finish school. I can go to school next year."

"This was not the plan," I say.

The amadlozi murmur on the opposite side of the room. I ignore them. I can't help wishing that sometimes they'd butt out. I can't help wishing that sometimes I had a choice about this, a choice to say, *No. Not right now. Come back in an hour or two.*

"Gogo dying was not the plan either," he says.

"What if you don't get a bursary next year?" I say.

"They tell me it will wait for one year," he says. "And besides, it is too late. I've already done it."

Perhaps now I should tell him that I have withdrawn from school. But I feel too much shame. He sacrificed it all, for me, and for what? For nothing. So I keep silent.

"What is the job?" I ask finally.

"I'm working for a taxi," he says, "collecting the money."

"But—"

He holds up his hand to stop me. "It's a good job," he says. "My route goes by your school, so we can take you in the mornings and again at night. See? And you won't have to pay. The driver will take it out of my wages."

"Little Man," I say.

He puts his arm around me and cuddles me against his shoulder. "Shhh," he says. "Don't say anything. The only thing I want to do is help you and Zi. That is all."

It would be so wonderful to feel like I'm not alone. To know that Little Man and I—

And soon we're kissing again and the kissing keeps going and…and… We've never had time like this. Gogo is always around or Zi.

I should stop this.

I melt into his arms.

I should stop this…but…

His lips march up my arm to my neck, little ants nibbling. He nips my collarbone, uses his tongue to lick the skin down down down. His fingers caressing the small of my back, inching their way up my shirt and gently trailing across my waist. An explosion of birds flapping in my stomach and heart and…

Khosi. A warning from Gogo.

Not just now, Gogo.

You promised…

Yebo, Gogo, yebo. I've broken one promise and I'm about to break another. But this is not one you need to witness. You stay here. In the living room. Don't follow me.

"Little Man," I whisper.

He freezes. Lips puckered, about to kiss my nipple. Fingers gripping the extra flesh around my hips.

"Ngiyakuthanda, Khosi," he whispers, as though ashamed.

"I love you too," I whisper back.

Don't follow me, Gogo. Don't you dare follow me. And that goes for the rest of you too. Mkhulu. All you amadlozi. I don't need your judgments or your eyes on me. Stay here. All of you.

"Woza," I say. And lead him down the hallway to the bedroom.

CHAPTER SEVEN

THE PROBLEM OF JEALOUSY

And so begins our new life.

While Zi is at school, I open the gate and leave a sign that says I am available for customers. I wave hello at all the neighbors, even the ones who just look my way without responding because they believed all of Auntie's lies. But a sangoma has to be friendly to all the people…even though I really just want to sink into my own private world with Zi. It is hard to always put on a public face.

They say a prophet is never honored in her own country. How can my neighbors ever accept me as anything but little Khosi, the girl they saw grow up? How can they ever let me be this thing among them—a sangoma, a voice for the ancestors? And how will they ever get over all the suspicion and lies that my aunt spread?

Once the gate is open and the sign is out, I wait.

Well, I sort of wait. I can't keep still for long, so I make some tea with lots of hot milk and sugar. I drink it slowly. Then I examine Gogo's garden. It is looking pretty scraggly, so I water it carefully and then look for weeds to pull.

"What do you think, Nhlanhla?" I ask. "Should we start a new garden?"

Nhlanhla crouches at the foot of a tall, bedraggled mealie plant and barks.

"Yebo, I agree," I say. "Let's start over. Tomorrow, we'll hike up into the hills and find some plants that we can transplant. Winter herbs…"

It's cold outside so I light a fire in the hut and Nhlanhla lies down beside me. We look at the fire, at the smoke curling upwards, and I start to drift into a sweet, sleepy haze.

"Makhosi?"

I jerk awake. A young man has entered the hut, smiling, flashing white teeth at me. Nhlanhla's tail thumps loudly on the floor.

I've decided to keep Nhlanhla beside me whenever I'm seeing customers. She stays in the hut by my side and growls if somebody gets too close. I don't want to be unwelcoming but twice in the first week, two of the men who visited me thought that because I'm a young woman, they could get more than what they requested. But they underestimated the protection of my ancestors.

The first man left with a hole in the seat of his pants and a fresh dog bite on his rear end.

The second man was shocked when a snake started slithering towards him, fangs wide, glistening with poison.

I haven't been bothered since then but it's early days yet. I keep Nhlanhla beside me all the time. I'm not taking any chances. I like to think Gogo's spirit passed into her and sometimes, I swear, I see Gogo looking at me through her amber-brown eyes. Or I hear Gogo's voice in her whine.

Not that I need Nhlanhla to hear your voice, Gogo. God forbid that you should ever shut up.

It's reassuring, in this case, that Nhlanhla simply wags her tail and does not move. She keeps her eyes trained on the young man but otherwise, she is at peace.

"Welcome," I say. "Please sit."

"Thank you, Makhosi." He sits to the side of me and nervously picks at the collar of his shirt. He looks uncomfortable. He keeps running a finger around the inside of his collar.

"What do you need?" I ask.

"I am looking for a job," he says. "But I am afraid."

"What are you afraid of?"

He bows his head, ashamed. "I am afraid somebody has cursed me, to prevent my success."

I light impepho and begin to hum as the scent swirls around us. The young man's ancestors can hardly sit still, like eager and overactive children. They have been dying to speak to him for some time now and this is their first chance. I begin to ask the young man questions about his life so they can tell me what is wrong.

"Are you working already? Do you have a job?"

"I had a very good job, Makhosi, and some few months ago, I was laid off. I have been searching ever since with no luck."

"Do you have a wife?" I ask.

"Yes." He has a look of desperation on his face. "I have a beautiful wife. I paid a very high sum for her lobola. We have been married for two years yet and we do not have a child. She is worried. Why can't she fall pregnant? "

His ancestors murmur together. His great-great-grandmother looks agitated and begins to gesture as she whispers to the others. I catch a word here and there and slowly begin to see the whole picture.

"You have a twin brother," I say.

"Yes, Makhosi," he says.

"Is he married?"

He shakes his head.

"Your brother is very jealous," I say. "It seems he has always wanted what you have."

Drops of sweat gather at his temples and roll down his face and then neck. "I know this, Makhosi, but is he the one behind this?"

"The amadlozi seem to think so," I say. "It seems he wants your wife and is seeking to destroy your success so that you lose her."

He rubs his arms and shivers. He looks more sick and afraid than angry. "I have seen him watching her," he says. "But I never thought—my own brother." His groans are low but powerful, coming from a deep place of agony.

I reach out and gently touch his shoulder. "It will be all-right, mfowethu. I will send some herbs for your wife to take that will help her to conceive or help prepare her body for pregnancy."

"Siyabonga, Makhosi, siyabonga."

"And for you, I will give you some muthi to cleanse your body and mind. And then I want you to know that your brother's curses cannot work, only if you believe them. You must talk to your brother. He is your family. The amadlozi do not like this thing of contention between the two of you. If you talk to him, you can work it out, and the power of those curses will dissipate. Like mist in the air."

He sighs, a hollow well of what was once fear and now is simply relief.

When he leaves with a packet of herbs and some of the water I have blessed and instructions to return to me when he has found a job and his wife conceives, I take a moment to pray for him. I pray to the amadlozi and also to the Lord of the Skies. It is not easy, what he must do. It would be easier just to take the medicine and think everything will be solved, but no. Dissension of this kind, it will only be solved if he confronts his brother.

I never had that chance with Mama. She died before I could tell her how angry I am with her—for stealing money from our neighbor, for refusing to take medicine for her HIV so that she ended up dying. I have tried to make peace with it, and to forgive her, but I wonder sometimes if I have succeeded. She is restless, she wanders back and forth among the amadlozi, never speaking to me; I also never speak to her and I too feel as though I can never rest. I must go here, go there, seeking something. But what?

Plenty sits still but hunger is a wanderer. And I am hungry.

CHAPTER EIGHT

Afraid Things will Change, Afraid They'll Stay the Same

Zi stands before me, a certain begging in her eyes. It's not that what she wants—money for some little what what what that is all the big rage at school—is such a big deal. But I'm barely holding on as it is, trying to pay for everything we need.

"Don't be like the hyenas," I tell her, "the ones who go after the lion's leavings."

Her eyes tell me that I am a lioness, she is my cub, and therefore she doesn't need to be a hyena, she simply needs to wait until I get hungry enough to provide. But she says nothing.

"Now get ready for school," I say, "or you will be late. Little Man's taxi is coming now now to take you. In fact, I already received a text saying he is on his way to meet you."

She hurries into her uniform, a white shirt and green skirt, the same uniform I wore every day before I had to quit. I miss it, all of it. It's a quiet ache in the back of my throat—always there but barely felt now.

Zi shrugs a coat over her uniform, and then her backpack with her school things. We head outside, locking the door and the gate, even though Little Man's khumbi will come right to the corner to pick her up, within sight of the house.

But locking up is something I do religiously. Yes, yes, I placed a charm around my place to ward off thieves. Of course, my ancestors will do what they can to keep the place safe. But I still lock up. That's good sense. If nothing else, training to become a healer has taught me the limits of my powers. I can put a protective hedge around my house but I cannot guarantee that evil will not find a way in. I will never be one of these sangomas that passes out pamphlets in city squares, promising miracles. If people come to me, I will do what I can, the best I can do— the best my ancestors give me in any given circumstance. Sometimes what I have to give them will work. Sometimes what I have to give them will fail. That is all. No guarantees. No false promises.

But the real truth is that sometimes people ask for one thing when it is something else they actually need. And they aren't always happy to learn this.

The morning is cold enough to see our own breath. Smoke rises from fires in yards as we walk past fences along the dirt road towards the taxi rank. A blue haze hovers low in the horizon, the landscape dotted with houses lining the zigzag streets and going up into the hills in the distance. A flock of squat brown Hadeda jubilate across the road, greeting the morning with joyous squawks.

Little Man's waiting for us at the corner, sitting on the stone that people use as a bench, hunching into his black hoody against the cold wind. "Hey, Khosi," he greets me.

"Hey, Little Man." My voice is still rough with leftover dreams from the long night.

He takes my hand and kisses the palm with his lips, soft soft, and I shiver, just like the first time he kissed me. His calloused hand gently caresses mine, holding it as though he's holding me. I admit, his presence makes me feel safe. Calm. And I wonder if I could, or should, finally tell him yes. Yes to what he wants. To what he keeps asking me. *Yes, come live with us. Yes, let's be together, always.*

But I keep telling him no. Despite everything. Even though I've already broken my promises to Gogo, that feels like it would take it one step too far.

"Hello, little Zi." Little Man and Zi slap palms in a high five.

She's so tiny, he's able to lift her across his shoulders and carry her like a bag of mealies. She giggles and kicks her legs and finally cries, "Let me down, Little Man!" so he swings her back down and places her gently on the ground.

"Someday, I'm going to carry you all the way to town that way," he threatens.

She sticks her tongue out at him and he laughs.

"Maybe I'll just carry your older sister to town instead." His eyes appraise me, those eyes that say so much more than the words. "Do you think I could carry you over my shoulder, Khosi?" he asks.

I blush and look at the ground. I won't answer, he already knows, but he loves to tease me like this.

"Khosi's bigger than you," Zi informs Little Man, as if he didn't know that already.

"I know." He wiggles his eyebrows at me. "She's perfect."

"Stop it, Little Man," I say weakly, looking all around to see if anybody is watching and listening.

"Oh, now, we're embarrassing her," Little Man tells Zi. "We better stop before we both get in trouble."

They look at me with such pitiful expressions, I have to start laughing. Little Man elbows Zi and they grin at each other and then at me. I shake my head at them. "You are *too much* crazy."

"We are *too much* wonderful," Zi says. She leans into Little Man and he puts an arm around her. It reminds me for some few seconds of how much she's lost—and I'm that glad Little Man has been in our lives these past three years. And that he is here still.

"Khosi, hey! I sent you some customers yesterday," Little Man says.

"What did they need? What were they looking for?"

"They didn't say."

"Did you tell them to go to hospital?" I try to think like this: medicine first, then Zulu medicine. But I don't always succeed. Being a sangoma is my livelihood, after all, and my dream of becoming a nurse is only getting further and further away, especially now that I had to quit school. So sometimes the Zulu ways seem more important to me…they are certainly more important now now, with my need to make money.

"They were coming from Edendale already," he says. "She'd just been released. She had medicine but she wasn't happy with the diagnosis. She said something about a relative that was angry with her and she thinks that relative may be practicing witchcraft against her... She has tried many things to get better and nothing works."

I nod, grateful that he's sending people my way.

"Bo's here," Zi announces, pointing to the white and tan khumbi that jerks to a stop at the corner. Bo, Little Man's boss, waves the two of them over, a wordless hurry up.

Swiftly, Little Man reaches out, grips my waist to pull me close. He kisses me so sweetly, my whole body tingles. "Goodbye, S'thandwa," he says tenderly and holds a hand out to Zi. "Ready, Zinhle?" he asks.

She takes his hand and they board the empty mini-bus, which will soon fill with passengers.

Little Man works for Bo seven days a week, long hours—it seems like twelve hours a day. Bo drives the taxi and Little Man collects money from the passengers.

It feels like we hardly see him anymore. Well, Zi sees him, to and from school.

He works so many hours because he's saving up. He decided he wants to buy his own taxi and be his own boss. When I ask him about the bursary, and going back to school, he just shakes his head.

Still, even if I wish it was different, I couldn't do it without his help. He arranged his long hours so he could start when Zi needs to go to school and he accompanies her. They drop her off at the front door of the school. He's still working when school is over so his taxi swings by the school and picks her up at the corner, and he makes sure she comes safely home too. They're always there to pick her up on time, none of this "five minutes, five minutes" business, which can mean an hour or even longer. I can't even say how grateful I am for his thoughtfulness and care, since I can't take her myself. Plus, he refuses to let me pay the fare. So there's that too. Every rand I save counts.

He was angry when he learned that I had quit school without borrowing school fees from him first—but he doesn't understand. I can't be *that* in debt to anybody for anything. Even Little Man.

Sometimes I think I'd be happier if I sold the house and we moved to Durban, if I started up my healing practice there instead of here. Zi could go to a good school in Durban. Since water is the main healing tool or power the ancestors gave me, it would be nice to be near the warm, salty seas of the Indian Ocean.

But the thing about the ancestors is that they tell you where to go and whenever I think Durban, they say, *No no no no*. Or, sometimes, *Not yet*.

Plus, and this is a big thing, I must think about Little Man too. He's an Imbali man through and through. I don't see him leaving this place ever. After all, he wants to establish his own taxi business! Of course, I haven't given him a chance to say he might be willing to move. I haven't talked to him about what I want to do. I don't even know why. Sometimes I'm afraid things will change. Sometimes I'm afraid things will stay the same forever and ever.

Maybe if I'd moved away as soon as Gogo died, like I wanted, I wouldn't be in so much trouble now. Because something's happened that I can't take back… But then I have to wonder—is this thing that happened also the reason they keep telling me no no no? Is it too late to leave?

Tell me, Gogo. Did I make just that one wrong decision and ruin my future plans forever?

I hope not. But it's possible. I might just be stuck here in Imbali… forever.

CHAPTER NINE

MEDICINE OF A SORT

After sending Zi to school, I stop at the tuck shop and part with a few precious rands for a cool drink.

The tuck shop on my street used to be owned by a man who lived just next door to the shop. But he sold it to a Somali family some few months back. Occasionally, the wife is here, wearing her long skirts and bright red or pink head coverings, her children hovering in the background, sucking thumbs or candy and staring at me. But most of the time, the husband runs the shop. I don't know where they live but it's not in Imbali—I'm sure they live far from here, probably because they worry all the time that they will be attacked. Now we slide rands through a small hole in an iron grid meant to protect the man inside from weapons. That's because he's already been robbed at gunpoint twice, and he's only been in Imbali for six months!

The Somali-run tuck shop isn't the only change in Imbali. A Chinese herb and healing center opened just a short, ten-minute walk from my front door. Makhosi says not to worry. "Even if people try this Chinese stuff," she says, "they'll always come back to sangomas. Nothing can replace hearing from your own loved ones who have passed on to the other side. You think those Chinese healers can hear our dead? No, they may have magic herbs but you must be Zulu to do what we do."

Even if they don't hear our ancestors' voices, people are seduced by the Chinese: they respect healers who have come from a long ways away. It seems like people believe that the farther away it comes from, the better it must be.

At least, when it comes to medicine.

They don't feel that way about Somalis or Chinese who own tuck shops and grocery stores. I don't blame this man for putting up bullet proof sliding where he takes the money, or keeping himself locked in all the time. It wasn't so long ago that people dragged Somalis through the streets in Durban, killing them for no other reason than that they run the tuck shops so, according to the people, they must be taking away jobs from South Africans.

I greet the man in Zulu, "Sawubona, Ahmed, nina ninjani?" Then in Arabic, "As-salaam 'alaykum." I want him to know that he has nothing to fear from me. I'm perfectly OK with his presence here in the township. No matter how different—or similar—he is.

Ahmed nods and smiles at me, sliding a Coke through the opening. "Are you doing well today, sister?" he asks. He has a deep voice, the kind I imagine Little Man having someday, when he's a little older. I've known Little Man since before his voice changed and every year it gets deeper.

"Yebo, bhuti, the day is just beginning," I say. "Wish me luck for my business."

"What is your business, sister?"

I try to think about how to translate what I do for people who are not Zulu. "I pray for people. I pray to the Great Lord of the Sky and also to our ancestors, all of our ancestors, to help me discern what is causing their illness and what they need to make them well again. Then I give them herbs or holy water to heal their sickness and I bless them so that their health is good."

The way his hair looks, soft and springy, is different than Zulu hair. But the darkness of his skin—not yellow-black, like most of us—reminds me of Little Man's blue-black tones. "I was myself a doctor in my own country before I came here," he says. "And we too have our healing traditions in Islam."

"What are they?" I ask.

"We have many. In some parts of the world, an imam will write the words of the Qu'ran on paper and a sick person will swallow the holy words to make themselves well again. Or they may wear a protective amulet to prevent or heal sickness."

I look at him again, closer this time. "And as a doctor," I say, choosing my words carefully, "what do you think of these traditions?"

He spreads his arms wide as if embracing the world. "They cannot do harm," he says. "And they may do good. I trust that Allah is good and means the best for all of us. We say in Islam that there is no illness for which Allah hasn't created a cure. And so I pray for my patients and I also give them good medicine, the best I know how, to make them well again."

It is not so different from how I practice Zulu medicine then.

He looks sad. "Or at least, I used to do all of that. Now I dispense Coca-Cola products, bread, and biscuits."

"It is important work," I say, meaning to comfort him. "Many of us depend on you. It is hard to get to the Spar or Checkers and it is too much expensive to shop there. You help us get our daily bread. That is medicine of a sort." Of course, now that the new shopping center opened next to Imbali, it is easier to get to a grocery store—but accessible does not mean affordable. And some elderly people have trouble getting even that far. Shame, we should have a service for that. Some man on a bicycle could fetch and deliver food for them.

He shrugs. Here is a man who feels thwarted. He fled his country and saved his life but his soul is drying up, withering away. What a terrible thing it must be to leave your home and everything you love just because you must save your physical life.

I wonder if he felt called by Allah to be a doctor? If, like me, he realized the gift he had been given wasn't of his own choosing but something he must do? Then how hindered he must feel now. Does he still feel the pulsing need in his hands to heal? The voice in his head that tells him, Do this, do that, save them?

Yes, I see from the pain in his eyes, he still feels it, and it has no release. No release in this bread and fruit, the gum and cigarettes, that he must push from one side to the other in exchange for money. Some calling indeed. I wish I could relieve him of this need. Let him know that others are taking up the burden. Like me. But I know that will not solve this thing for him. When you feel called, and then you are thwarted—it is a terrible thing.

"Sister," he says, pushing a small chocolate into my hands, "may you have a good day for business inshallah."

I pocket the chocolate as a treat for Zi later. "And you too, bhuti."

Nhlanhla greets me with hysteric barks as I approach the house, as if I've been gone for days. I rub her behind her ears and speak in a soothing voice until she calms down. She licks my hand with wild abandon as I slip inside.

What would I do without her?

I open the gate wide and set out the sign, advertising my services. A woman old enough to be my mother is toiling up the hill to my house, waving a hand at me, so I wait until she arrives.

"Sawubona, Mama," I greet her. She grasps my arm and I help her inside, closing the gate and escorting her towards the traditional round hut in the back behind the main house.

She leans on me, her weight heavy. I help her sit, settling Nhlanhla beside me. She gulps the glass of water I give her, calming herself. Although this is what I do every day, and it is second nature, it is sometimes hard for people to approach sangomas and ask for help. They never know what they might hear, good or bad. Plus, I am young. Sometimes they don't want a young woman who could be their daughter or granddaughter knowing the truth.

"What is your surname, Mama?" I ask her.

"Nene," she says.

"And your first name?"

"Gladys."

"And what are you seeking, Mama?"

"Protection," she says. "I have heard you know how to protect yourself…so for this thing, I am seeking help from you."

"Protection from who or what?" I ask.

She shakes her head. She doesn't want to name it.

It's not important. Her Nene ancestors—or my own grandfather Mkhulu—will tell me what I need to know. That's the thing the people don't know: how much more I know than what they tell me.

"Do you believe you've been cursed? Does someone wish to harm you?"

"No," she says. "But my boys may call a curse down upon us."

"What do you mean?"

"No good can come with the things they are doing," she says. "Angaz', I thought I raised them to be good boys. But now they're sniffing around that Somali's tuck shop. They say foreigners don't belong here, not in Imbali. They say they're going to do something."

She grabs my hand. "I'm afraid, ndodakazi, afraid. What are they doing? What if they hurt that man? Will I suffer because of what they do?"

The desperation in her grip strikes fear in my heart. But I pretend to be calm. "I will ask the ancestors to protect you," I say, "and to keep your boys from doing anything they should not do."

I smudge the room with impepho, humming gently. Calling to Mkhulu. Calling to this woman's ancestors. Then I settle myself on the floor beside her and close my eyes. Immediately, bright images thud through my mind like loud music, doof doof doof, one after the other.

Two lions chasing after a gazelle.

The gazelle's body, broken and mangled, lying in the dirt.

A pool of blood mixing with earth.

A woman screaming.

A prison, tall and grey, on a city street, the sounds of sobbing men seeping through the closed windows.

I open my eyes quickly, to free myself of the images. But the woman is still there before me, neck bent, and I must say something. I can tell her the truth, or I can soothe her, or I can tell her the truth while trying to soothe her. What do I do? What do I do, Mkhulu?

The woman keeps her head bent but her eyes sweep upwards as she peeks at me, a soft swift cunning, and in that little movement, I know. I know everything. She isn't coming to stop something. No. She's coming because she doesn't want to be punished or suffer consequences for what they have done and what they plan to do. She's seeking absolution in advance.

"*What are your boys going to do?*" I ask. My voice is low but stern, not a voice I would or should use with an elder but suddenly, I am her elder, I am thousands of years older than her, as I speak in the voice of all the people that have gone before us. "You are afraid but you already know they are up to no good. They are already stealing and hurting strangers among us. What more will they do?"

She stands suddenly, sobbing, and I reach out to her, like I would anybody who is sorrowing, but something stops me hard. As though my grandfather Mkhulu has blocked my hand.

"Please, I need protection," she yells.

Something cold and horrible grips my stomach. "Cha! You will never receive the protection of your ancestors."

"Why not?" she cries.

"It is said, 'Do not call a dog with a whip in your hand.' You know we must take pity on the stranger and be kind. You cannot ask for protection as long as you do nothing to stop your boys, as long as you provide them with a home and a safe place to hide while they go and shame you, while they go and shame all Zulus. Or if you take money from them. Mama, you cannot ask for protection from the ancestors if you are accepting blood money from your sons."

She jerks away, as though my words burn.

The beads on my headpiece rattle and clang as I shake my head at her. "You tell your sons that I'm putting a protective charm over that man. You tell your sons to leave him alone or they will regret it."

Her lips curl into a sudden sneer. "What would you know about it anyway?" she asks. "You, you with everything? Go on now and tell an old lady she should starve."

The words sear my lips. "When did it become a battle between starvation and doing the right thing?"

"You wouldn't understand," she yells. "I have nothing, only my sons."

"Go do what is in your heart to do," I say. "And if you do the *right* thing, the ancestors will protect you, with or without my help."

She hurries out of the room, weeping.

Eish, that's one way to make sure I don't get paid.

Next time, ask for payment before you tell her the truth, Mkhulu chides me. He has a deep chuckle that echoes around the room.

It's not funny, I tell him. If I don't earn money, Zi and I don't eat.

I'm already thinking about the empty cupboards in the house. But a half loaf is better than no bread. At least there's a full sack of mealies so I can make phuthu with some spinach growing in the garden.

Gogo planted that spinach before she died and it's flourished, thank you, Gogo, along with some few small herbs, thank you, amadlozi. I'll have to learn, with their help, how to garden next year. In addition to food, I must also plant a garden full of herbs to use for medicines.

Nhlanhla follows me out to the front yard. We stand at the gate and watch the woman's retreating back as she runs home fast fast. She's calling out to somebody as she passes, probably telling them not to visit the rude young sangoma in Unit J.

I look at the tuck shop across the way. Ahmed struggles to take down a sign announcing oranges for five rand. Two young men saunter past, staring. What has happened to us? Gogo told me in the old days, those young men would be ashamed if they didn't offer assistance. Now they just stare.

Sighing, I command Nhlanhla to stay and walk briskly to Ahmed's side to help him with the sign.

His mouth parts in a startled smile. He has a gap between his teeth. "Ngiyabonga," he thanks me in his accented Zulu.

"Pleasure," I say. Then, in a hurry, "I feel I should warn you, bhuti."

He takes a step back. "Warn me? Is it?"

"Some people in Imbali wish harm to you."

"What?" His voice is too loud and his eyebrows draw together, both angry and confused.

My stomach can't handle all the tension—between the old woman and now Ahmed. Bile rises in my throat and I swallow it back. It stings as it goes back down the esophagus.

"I do not think you are safe here," I say. "You must take care. Protect yourself."

He starts backing up, heading inside, afraid, as though I'm threatening him rather than warning him.

I hold my hands out to show I mean no ill. "I hear things," I say. "Please be careful. Please!"

He's already inside the tuck shop, slamming shut the opening where people pay and receive their goods. "Go," he says when he sees me standing there. "Go now. Please. Just go. Go away."

As I lean over to vomit in the dirt, I wonder if I should have kept my mouth shut. And I forgot to tell him that I would pray for him.

I wipe my mouth and stand beside Nhlanhla. We watch as he closes shop, gets in his bakkie, and drives away, leaving a cloud of dust behind him. He doesn't look at me again.

I wonder if he'll be back, and if he comes back, whether he'll bring protection: other people or a gun. I imagine he prays to Allah, as Muslims do. I hope Allah will help him, protect him, just as the amadlozi and God help me. I hope he comes back because without the tuck shops, the people of Imbali hurt.

But I have a moment of foreboding as Nhlanhla and I make our way back to the hut, waiting for our next customer. A dark cloud on the horizon.

Something evil is on its way to Imbali. Like the rain that falls, it will touch all of us.

CHAPTER TEN

War

Little Man's taxi is late. I wait at the taxi rank as I do each day to fetch Zi. There's always some variation in the arrival time, of course, but today they are too much late.

All of the taxis are late.

I move closer to a group of gogos waiting for their grandchildren, just as Gogo used to do.

Oh, Gogo, I miss you.

The group of elderly women is rustling around, grumbling, keeping the worry out of their voices by acting irritated. One of them meets my eyes, then looks away, afraid when she sees that I also am worried.

I forget, sometimes, that I'm not just a neighborhood granddaughter anymore. Now I'm a link to the other world. I'm supposed to *know things*. If I'm calm, everything must be all-right. If I'm worried, then I must *know something*. Even if the truth is that I worry because I'm human, just like they do—not because the ancestors have warned me that something bad is about to happen.

It makes me want to scream sometimes that my gift doesn't work like that. It is not as though I know everything.

As far as the amadlozi goes, it's a one-way line of communication. I can ask ask ask ask ask and they can choose to be silent. But if they want something? They will not shut up, not for a second, not until I do what they say.

That is something that the ancestors do not tell you when they call you to be a sangoma. This thing that you are, it is not an enviable position. As a sangoma, you are the guardian of secrets in your community. It puts you in danger, actually. Sometimes, you know these secrets because the people themselves come and tell you. Sometimes, you know these secrets because the ancestors tell you something, something you wish you did not know. You may know half-secrets or you may know full-secrets but either way, you walk around with this heavy burden that you cannot be rid of. But other times, people think you know something, and you do not. And they look at you or they look away, either way because they are afraid of you. They avoid you. They try to harm you. They hide. They do whatever they can to keep you from seeing them.

If I had known all this, I might have told Mkhulu no when he called me to this life, though I do not see how you tell a dead person no.

That is also my problem with Gogo. With a breathing person standing in front of you, blood running through their veins, you can explain that what they asked you to promise is now impossible, or was not a reasonable or even responsible thing for them to ask. With a person who is gone, you can only tell their spirit, and their spirit does not care how impossible it is. Spirits are not something you can reason with. They want only what they want and nothing else will satisfy.

One of the gogos stops in front of me. She takes my hands in her own. "Are they all-right, Makhosi?" she asks.

"Who?" My eyes cross with confusion and worry as I look beyond her to the taxi rank, hoping to see Little Man's taxi careening towards us the way it does, always a little off center and just that much too fast.

"Our children," she says. "Our babies."

"Oh, yes, yes," I say, hurried. Because they are OK. But I'm not sure if Little Man is, or if Zi is. But these women? This time, I think they have nothing to fear. But if the evil I'm sensing is real and true, we all have something to fear in the coming months. "Just now, they are OK."

Her whole body relaxes and she turns away, joy in her face and on her lips, and then the other women are shouting their joy, and I turn away because I can't bear it all.

The white and tan taxi that Little Man works for tears recklessly down the potholed road and jerks to a stop right in front of me. And I just stare. Because it's pockmarked with bullet holes.

Little Man hustles off and shoves Zi in my direction. "Try not to worry," he yells in my direction, "I will call later! It's a bit hectic just now!" And then his taxi streaks off down the road again.

Zi's crying, holding her stomach.

The gogos surround us. One of them pats her back. Another pats her arm. Little Man's taxi disappears around a curve, the road empty now.

The gogo I spoke with earlier glances at me, a slight look of accusation on her face, and I snap because I can't help it, "Your babies are fine, I promise."

A few seconds later, several khumbis pull up in the normal fashion and, just as I said, the gogos' grandchildren pile off, in no hurry and with no worries. The gogos acknowledge me with a slight nod and then they head down the road with their grandchildren.

I take Zi's hand and we walk home. I don't ask what happened. I know once Zi is ready, the words will come pouring out of her mouth like a sudden October rain and she won't stop talking.

Sure enough, as soon as we sit down for a cup of tea, Zi puts her little brown hand on mine. "Please don't be mad at me, Khosi," she says.

"Never!" I say, even though we both know that's a lie. Now that I'm her mama, I get mad at her all the time. But that's her own fault. If she was just a little more thoughtful...less heedless... But a leopard can't scrub off its spots, nor a lion shave its own mane.

Her eyes twinkle at me. At first, I think it's because she's laughing but actually, her eyes are shedding tears.

"Another khumbi pulled up next to ours," she says. "First we were laughing and Little Man told Bo to race them. So we started speeding up. And then, the next thing, two of the men on that khumbi were pulling out guns and they were pointing them at us and *shooting*."

I jump up at Zi's words and stand at the window, the one that looks out on the road that leads into town. It's too late to see Little Man's khumbi drive past, of course—he's long gone—but that's what I'm straining for, a glimpse of it, just one last sign to know that he's safe, at least for the moment.

So the taxi wars have started again.

When I was younger, about Zi's age, there was a terrible taxi war—not just in Imbali but in all the townships around Pietermaritzburg. Because taxi routes are not organized by the city government but by private taxi owners, anybody who controls them is guaranteed a good income. For months, taxi drivers in one association shot at taxi drivers in another association. They hijacked taxis at gunpoint, beat up competitors, and held customers hostage. All of them were trying to gain control of different taxi routes. They were little more than gangsters. And it tore the township to bits. Taxi drivers died. Innocent people died. Children died.

If another taxi war has started, everybody is in danger. Most of all, Little Man. If a taxi war has started, can he remain the gentle man I've grown to love? No. He must leave this job. He must.

I pound my hand on the table so hard, little tendrils of pain shiver up and down my arm.

"Are you angry?" Zi asks.

I whirl around. It's not just her tiny, little-girl voice that makes her seem so small. Poor little Zi, always shorter and smaller than other little girls her age. She may be nine but she looks like she's only six or seven. "I'm not angry at you, Zi," I sigh. "But I'm angry, yes. Why is life so impossible? How can I let you get on another khumbi? How are you going to get to school?"

"I have to go to school, Khosi," Zi says. "But I'm scared."

I pull her towards me to hug her. "We'll figure something out."

Even as I say it, my head screams no. How can Zi go to school if the taxi wars have started again? I can't risk her life every morning, every afternoon. But how can she stay home? If she does, the state may come and say I cannot keep her.

"We will get up early," I start to plan out loud. "We'll walk. And then I'll return to get you."

"You will spend all day walking," Zi says. "And then have no time to work. We'll have to leave before it's light outside and come home after dark. Will we be safe?"

I knew it was a bad idea as soon as I spoke it out loud but I have to think. *Think, Khosi.*

"I will spend a great deal of time walking, it is true," I say. "But not all day. And for now, we have no other choice."

I sit in bed beside Zi, wrapped in blankets, a hot-water bottle wrapped in a towel and placed at our feet to keep us warm. The cold house is quiet, as though it, too, is listening. I'm waiting still to hear from Little Man. The minutes pass and I begin to envision his khumbi riddled with bullet holes, Little Man splayed on the hard ground, bleeding from fatal gunshot wounds.

Stop it, Khosi, I chide myself in as stern a voice as I can muster.

The phone rings once, sharply. Little Man! But as soon as I pick it up and say hello, the line is already dead.

Wouldn't it be horrible if he'd called to say goodbye just now and that was his final phone call ever? My last vision is the khumbi pulling away, half of Little Man's body inside and half out, as he shouted at me, promising to call later.

A few minutes later, the phone rings again. I jump up and take my phone into the hallway and out to the kitchen. I look out the window at my neighbors' house and the sea of orange-yellow lights burning in the night.

"Sorry, Khosi." Little Man sounds breathless. "We must be quick quick."

"You're OK?"

"Ehhe."

I hadn't realized I was holding my breath until he says this. I let it out in a small, controlled whoosh, hoping he doesn't hear it. "Are you home? Are you safe?"

"Ehhe," he says.

"Don't lie to me."

"OK, OK." He laughs and I picture him holding his hands defensively in the air, as if to ward off my words. "I'm not home yet but I'm almost there. I'm walking up the hill to my house. If you go out into your front yard, I'll see you."

I unlock the front door and go out onto the front stoop.

"I'm waving at you," he says.

In the distance, on the hill towards Little Man's house, a blurry blob is moving around. I'm guessing that's Little Man. I wave back.

"I can see you," he says. "Can you see me?"

"Yes," I lie.

"Are you and Zi safe?"

"Of course," I say.

I start to add, "But we're not OK—" except he interrupts with such a strong declaration: "*Good.* If you're OK, I can sleep then. If you need me—"

So I—well, I lie again. "We'll be fine," I say.

"All-right, I'm starting to walk again. I'll be safe just now, promise. I can see the light that Mama keeps on for me."

I decide to push him a little bit. "What about tomorrow? Will you be safe tomorrow? Or will there be more guns? Is there a war?"

"We don't know. It was Langa's men. They chased us off. We can only show up tomorrow and see what happens."

Langa is a big big man in Imbali. He owns twenty khumbis. Yes, he would do this, to regain control.

"What did Bo say?" Bo is his boss man.

"He said it can't happen again."

"What does *that* mean?"

Little Man is silent.

I make my question more specific: "Is he bringing a gun with him? Are you going to fight back?"

"I don't know."

I wanted Little Man to say it himself. To say, if it means a taxi war, I'll quit my job. I don't want to push him to say it. But—

"No," I say. "No guns. Please, Little Man, promise me." My voice is shrill and high, demanding—not the way I wish to be with him. But I can't control it. "Let's talk about this. Let's make a plan. Let's—"

"S'thandwa, sweetheart." His voice is low, countering mine, placating.

I picture him facing his house, the single lightbulb next to his mother's door shining out in the night to welcome him home. "You know it isn't my khumbi, Khosi MaKhosi. I don't make the decisions. Bo is my boss."

I take deep breaths.

"What can I do?" he asks and waits for my answer.

Little Man is not like some men, filling the silences with words just so that it isn't awkward. I am silent a long time. I walk from the kitchen to the bedroom and gaze down at Zi, sleeping in the bed we share. She used to share this bed with Gogo. Now I share it with her and my own bed, the one I shared with Mama until she died three years ago, is in the living room, our make-shift sofa.

I want to force Little Man's hand, make him promise not to go to work tomorrow, but I know that would be stupid. He's either going to make this choice or not. And then there will be another choice. And I also have choices. I do not believe this thing of fate or destiny. It is your destiny to make choices. *Good* choices.

"Don't come for Zi in the morning," I say, trying to make my voice steady.

"Khosi?" He sounds surprised, like maybe I'm breaking up with him.

I hurry to add to my declaration so he doesn't read too much into it: "Come tomorrow when your work is over. You can tell me if it's safe. Then I will decide about Zi."

He starts breathing again as though my earlier words had caused him to stop. "I will be there tomorrow. Khosi…"

"Yebo?"

"Will you ask Mkhulu to protect me?"

I laugh, not because it's funny but because, well, it's like he's asked me to breathe.

"I will ask," I reassure him. "But you should know that their protection is never a promise."

"Nothing is a promise," he says. "Even a promise."

What does he mean by that? I want to ask but I don't dare. We hang up and I watch the hillside he's walking up towards his house. His mother has indeed turned on a light. I can see it, shining out in the twilight.

For three years now, that light and that house have reminded me of my friendship with Little Man. Since Gogo died, it has made me feel as though I'm not alone. But now, I don't know. How will he respond to this problem, the taxi war? Will he resist—or join in? What kind of man is Little Man going to turn into? Can I trust that he will be the same man I fell in love with? Oh, I hope so. God, go with him. Keep him safe and make him strong. Let him be the Little Man I need him to be...

CHAPTER ELEVEN

Walking There and Back Again

I wake Zi while it's still dark. She yawns and starts to complain but shuts up when I give her a tall thermos full of milky sweet tea. We dress quickly, feed Nhlanhla, and leave just as the sun comes up, Imbali bathed in a soft orange light.

News of the taxi war has spread. We're not the only ones walking to town. Gardeners and domestic workers trudge ahead of us on their way to work, while some women haul heavy bags of jewelry and carved wooden animals on their trek to town, where they will spread their wares on blankets to sell in front of Freedom Square or the Tatham Art Gallery.

It makes me feel safer to follow the crowds, especially through the darkened streets.

Besides taking Zi to school, I have things I want to accomplish. Last week I saw a flyer in downtown Pietermartizburg advertising a talk on what it called "sangoma medicine and sustainable practices" at the university. If I have to drop Zi off at school, I can at least hear the talk and spend the day in the city.

I estimate a little over an hour's walk to Zi's school and I am right, just. We run the last half block to make it as the bells start ringing. Zi runs inside and I turn to go.

"Khosi Zulu," somebody calls. I turn around to see Beth, one of my former classmates. Her hair glints red in the sunlight. "What are you doing here?"

"I am dropping my sister off."

She jogs over, her face full of frank curiosity. "I heard you quit school."

The way she says that stings. "I did not quit," I say. The sting comes out in my words, I can see it in the way she draws back, away from me. I gentle my tone. It isn't her fault, after all. It's my own. "My grandmother died and I didn't have money for tuition."

"Khosi, they have scholarships available."

I shrug. I'm not going to share all the factors with a perfect stranger. Beth was always nice but you can tell just by looking at her that she doesn't know what life is really like for most of us. "Not for me," I say. I don't want to go into the details that, in fact, I did have a scholarship. But trying to keep my grades up while training to be a sangoma—and then when Gogo got sick and I was trying to care for her and Zi… Well, the end of the story is that I lost my scholarship. Zi's still on scholarship…but I barely had enough to pay her extra fees.

Her eyes narrow. "You're smart. You could get one. You know any of the teachers in this school would recommend you."

I start inching my way off the sidewalk to cross the street. "It was really nice to see you, Beth. Good luck in school."

"I'm not letting this go, Khosi," she yells after me. "You were the best science student in our grade. You should be in school. I heard you gave it all up and for what? To be a sangoma? Shame!"

I flutter my hand at her and make my escape.

Does she mean shame that I had to give up school?

Or is she saying shame that I'm a sangoma? She's white but many white South Africans believe in this thing of African science and medicine. They have seen the power of muthi. Some of them have African ancestors, even if they didn't want to admit it during the time of apartheid.

"At least talk to the headmaster," she calls. "At least talk to him! Don't just give up!"

The university is still looking disheveled from some of the student protests this past week. Ripped signs litter the lawn in front of the clock tower. A burn spot on the pavement marks the grave of a random car that student protesters set fire to. Students have been agitating against the high fees they must pay to go to university. I understand what they are saying, I do. But I can't even pay the fees to matriculate. I'd like that chance first—to finish all my classes, to take my exams, to prove that I am worthy of the first of many diplomas. Maybe I should start protesting the fees just to finish school before even going to university!

The campus is quiet today. Maybe people are still staying home, afraid of what might happen. A couple of gogos zigzag across the front lawn, picking up ripped signs and garbage and putting it all in large plastic bags.

I ask one of them for directions and find the building I want, climbing the stairs to enter a classroom, almost empty because so few people dared to come. I'm surprised, after all, that they didn't cancel it. The talk has just started when I arrive so I take a seat near the back. Then I scan the people gathered here. Only one other sangoma is here, an older woman sitting in the middle of the room. We acknowledge one another.

The talk is…interesting. The speakers say that traditional medicine, as practiced, is ecologically unsound. Too many sangomas gather rare wild plants to the point that those plants are now endangered.

I understand the talk perfectly and I realize they're right. But it's one thing to say "sangomas should" do this and "sangomas shouldn't" do that and another thing to get a quarter million of us to do this thing they want us to do. The speakers are more sophisticated than that, of course, and use phrases like "using indigenous knowledge to conserve medicinal plants" or encouraging sangomas in the "propagation and cultivation" of medicinal plants rather than wild-harvesting so that what we do is "sustainable." But even if we cultivate the herbs we need, will that stop or reverse the destruction of the wild versions? This question is not asked or answered.

Also, there were so many things talked about that are not even a part of the medicine I trained in or now practice. For example, animal parts. I've met sangomas who use the parts of animals—a lion's foot, for example—but it is nothing I learned or would implement. That kind of medicine is usually for Other Things. Things we don't speak of. Things I would never do, though I've been accused of it. And of course, I've had close encounters with the witch that lives on the hill, the one that left me the goat. I'm sure she uses or has used animal parts. But if somebody came and asked me to do what what with animal parts, I'd tell them what what, believe me.

By the time I leave, I have a headache. I go to the front to talk with the young woman who spoke. "Did you spend time with sangomas?" I ask her.

"I did field research with three sangomas for six months," she replies smoothly and firmly.

Her spirit is closed. But I still have to say what I need to say.

"Every sangoma is different," I say. "We all practice our medicine differently because we have different ancestors. Not all of us gather wild herbs, or even the herbs you mentioned. Do you think you worked with enough sangomas to really understand what we do?"

"Yes, I believe I did. And I don't appreciate you questioning my research methodology." She looks beyond me to the next person. Dismissed!

I nod at her, briefly, and then walk away. She could have invited me to speak more openly. Perhaps she simply thought that I'm an opportunist. What do you think of that, hey, Mkhulu?

Still, even if she was rude, I could sense some truth in what she said to the audience, and something is beginning to burn deep in my belly in response to it all, but I'll have to think about it by myself. I still don't think she has the whole picture.

When I was in training, Mkhulu asked me to go to the ocean and bottle ocean water to bless. It required a long khumbi ride to Durban, a long walk to the sea, and a long khumbi ride home. It took all day. It certainly wasn't something I did for pleasure—I did it because I had to. A few times, he asked me to go to the Umgeni River, and once he asked me to go all the way to the mouth of the Thukela. I brought water back and I sprinkled that muthi all over our garden and our house, for protection and for blessing. I use it to this day.

Even now, I make some medicines with nothing but tap water and words. Maybe that's the Catholic part of me. Gogo, do you hear this? I may be struggling with this thing of God right now but it is still a part of me.

Water is not an everlasting resource, of course, but I think more sangomas could be trained this way. Of course, each sangoma follows the direction of their ancestors. Mine love water. I do too. It's cleansing and abundant. It can be polluted when you gather it but it's easy to purify through straining and boiling. And the body needs it to survive. Our bodies are, after all, at least half water. Water naturally purges the body of toxins.

Even though I was also trained in more traditional purging, the kind that causes people to vomit those things in their body or spirit causing their illness, I am not sure I will use that method. I suppose that means I'm not entirely traditional. That is, I've come to think of sangoma medicine as "adding to" rather than "subtracting from." Purging is subtraction rather than addition.

I myself nearly died, I think, when I used purging medications to expel evil from our lives just before Mama died. So it is not something I would recommend lightly. In fact, I have never once asked somebody to purge. I respect it, as needed—sometimes we must remove evil before we can replace it with goodness, similar to the way doctors must remove cancer. But I think water is just one example of a better way to flush the system of evil or toxins than by puking—which is not to say that sometimes the body reacts to spoiled food or poisons by expelling it. But that's a natural process of the body to protect it from harmful substances.

The talk ends while the day is still early and I have too much time before I have to pick up Zi from school so I wander around the university, pausing outside a laboratory. Posters on the walls and equipment identify this as a lab for the biological sciences.

My mind laps up the words on the posters, quick and so eager, and then I feel suddenly ill, like I consumed too much sugar all at once. I rush outside just in time to throw up.

One of the students sitting on the grass outside glances at me, askance or concerned, I'm not sure which. "Are you all-right?"

"I'm fine, just—sick."

"You shouldn't be here then," she says, demolishing any sense of sympathy. "You could get somebody else sick."

"You can't *catch* what I've got," I say, turning away and walking through the gates to the busy street beyond.

It's true, though, we speak about my condition and illness using the same words. People fall sick. I fell...

Well, Gogo, you know how I fell. But it is early yet. We cannot yet consider this thing to be settled.

Zi's school isn't far from the university so I walk there slowly, thinking. How can I find a way to go back to school? Is there a way to go to university without passing matric? Or is my life going to follow a different path? My stomach churns with this thought. Gogo, I don't wish to betray you or the promises I made.

I'm looking at the street ahead, just a tree-lined street of houses with green lawns hidden behind tall, electrified fences. But instead of houses and plants, I suddenly see Little Man, an uneasy smile on his face, gesticulating with his hands, talking talking talking—like he's pleading or perhaps trying to get himself out of a bad situation. And then he falls backward like something's knocked him over.

I rush forward to help him and find only empty streets. I glance around. A curtain flicks in one of the windows, the domestic help watching, wondering if I'm drunk or crazy.

My hand shakes as I take out my phone and dial his number. On the other end, it rings and rings, no answer.

I have little reason to talk on the way home. Inside my head, I'm chanting, *Mkhulu, keep him safe.*

Zi chatters away. She's telling me a story her history teacher told them today, one I've heard Gogo tell, about what happened when Chameleon ran afoul of God.

"Nkulunkulu told Chameleon to go and tell the people they would never die," Zi says.

I'm only paying half attention while I keep trying to reach Little Man on his phone. I try four times but each time, it does nothing but ring. I send a quick text: "Little Man, I'm worried. Call me please."

"But Chameleon got so distracted by some fruit he wanted that he never delivered the message," Zi says. "Nkulunkulu was angry, so he sent Lizard to tell the people that they would all die, they would all die indeed."

My attention is suddenly riveted to her worried face. "That story scares you."

She nods. "Everybody dies, Khosi."

"Zi," I say gently. "Don't you know how that story ends?"

"Yes, everybody dies," she repeats. "I already know that. First Mama, then Gogo, and next—you're not going to die next, are you, Khosi?"

I smile at her. "Listen, Zi, this is important. After God sent Lizard, what happened next?"

"The Chameleon reached the people with the message that they would not die, but he was too late. Lizard had already arrived with the message that the people would die." Zi sounds sullen. "So the people were angry and they killed Chameleon."

"Yes, exactly," I say. "The people killed him…they killed the bringer of good news! The same way the people killed Jesus. But the story doesn't say Chameleon was wrong. The last message is the one we should remember. *Lizard* said everybody would die. *Chameleon* said they would not. Which one was right? I say Chameleon is right! Haven't Zulus always believed in life after death?"

She nods slowly.

"So you see, death isn't the end of life. That's what I think the story says. People will die…but yet they will not die. They may leave earth but they just go on to something else. We don't know exactly what we will find when we go to the other side but we know we will be greeted by all our loved ones, the ones who have gone on before us. They are all there, waiting for us. Just remember, the lesson of the story is that the grave is not the end of life. It is just the beginning of another."

Even as I say this, even as I tell Zi this, I'm frantically dialing Little Man's phone number for a fifth time. Worried about what it means that he has not yet answered. Worried that he could be hurt or, worse, dead.

I didn't lie to Zi. I do believe that death is just another beginning. But I'm certainly not ready for Little Man to take *that* beginning on yet—that would mean the end of us, here, now.

Please let him answer, I beg God. *Now now.*

But yet again, he fails to answer. There is nothing to do except wait.

CHAPTER TWELVE

A Voice as Thin as the Sky

Even though Nhlanhla greets us with wild kisses, the house feels empty and cold when we arrive home. I sit in Gogo's cracked pink plastic chair by the kitchen door while Zi boils water for tea. Auntie didn't want this chair because it is old and ugly. But I'm glad to still have it.

When Gogo was alive, nobody sat in this chair except her. She used to sit here while I made dinner. You don't mind, do you, Gogo? Sitting in your chair makes me feel closer to you, like you're right here, in the flesh, not just in my head.

Tonight, dinner is a packet of biscuits and milky sweet tea, which we eat in the kitchen while the sky thins from blue to pink and then, finally, black, only the brightest of stars twinkling through Imbali's lights. We sit there, silent, until Zi says, "Khosi?" Her voice as thin as the sky.

I startle and sit up a bit straighter. "Yes, Zi?"

"Kwenzenjani?"

"I'm all-right." I hope by saying it, it will become true. "Let's see what's on TV." Maybe the noise and the light will be enough to chase this thing of too-much-thinking and too-much-worrying away.

If I could ask the amadlozi...but just now, Mkhulu and Gogo and the others offer only a deafening chorus of pure silence. That doesn't mean Little Man's OK. Nor does it mean Little Man's in danger. It means— well, exactly nothing. But I need to distract myself.

Someone rattles the gate. The fur on Nhlanhla's back sticks straight up and she growls, low but sure. I keep a hand on her as I peek out the window.

A very tall, very thin man stands just behind the gate.

Fear, a knife, slashes straight down my torso, from my throat to my stomach.

Though I have never spoken with this man, I recognize him. Langa, the taxi-driver with a fleet of taxis who controls so many of Imbali's taxi routes. During the bloody taxi-wars of my childhood, he was the man who rose to the top. Now he is the one going after Bo and Little Man's taxi route.

He stands upright, his body an arrow pointed toward the sky, carried with the kind of confidence you see only in men with real power. Though he's young enough to be my older brother, and handsome enough to make many women love him, his body bears evidence of his violent life, scars like tiny cobwebs spun across his hands, face, arms.

His own personal tsotsis slouch next to him, two young men I've seen around, one with the swagger of a boy who has done too much, the other looking to his friend for confidence. Soon, he will have too much of his own.

I have to wonder if they are just his bodyguards or if these thugs have plans for me.

I'm suddenly so angry at Little Man, my teeth hurt. Did he just send death to knock on my gate?

Well, if there is one thing I know, it is that death is a coward.

"Makhosi," Langa calls in a soft but persistent voice. "Makhosi." Makhosi, the name of respect given to sangomas, is also a word of desire. He wants something from me, needs something. Is power always like this? Does he also feel the sting of too much expectation from those who surround him?

Our eyes meet and even from this distance, I suddenly know and understand him. Yes, he could have me killed by snapping his fingers. But this man of so much apparent power actually controls very little. He must always do and be what others expect—like me. Like all sangomas. We're all trapped in our roles, in others' expectations.

Suddenly, I am no longer afraid. He can do what he wants with my body—but he actually has no power over me. Power is an illusion.

"Zi, lock this door and keep Nhlanhla with you," I say. "Watch through the window and call Little Man if anything scary happens, OK? Tell him Langa is here to visit me."

She nods quietly and watches as I slip out the door.

"Khosi," she hisses.

"What?" I stick my head back in the door.

"Please don't die," she says.

"I won't die," I say. But can anyone ever promise that? If death is a coward, after all, it means he'll make his move when your back is turned. Still, I am not afraid.

I take a deep breath and go outside. Langa immediately falls silent and watches me approach.

"Sawubona, Makhosi," he says.

"Sawubona," I greet him. "Nina ninjani?"

"Sikhona." He smiles and throws his arms wide to indicate his presence and that of the tsotsis beside him. Indeed, they are all here and they are all well. Then he jerks his head to the left and they step away, I suppose out of earshot.

"Why are you here?" I ask.

"I've heard that you offer strong protection," he says.

Even coming from a violent liar like Langa, I'll admit that I feel a strong burst of pride in my heart. I can't help the smile that creeps over my face.

"Word gets around," he says.

The nice fig is often full of worms, Khosi, Mkhulu whispers.

I stop smiling. "Why are you here?" I repeat.

"I need protection," he says.

"You? Why?" I ask.

Are you going to let him persuade you to help him? Gogo asks. She sounds puzzled. Incredulous. Don't do it, mtanami. Don't listen to him.

Oh, Gogo, do you really think I would help this man?

"From the evil men out to hurt me, out to take my business," he bursts out, fragile and childlike in his sudden fear and anger. "They're trying to kill me and take away everything I've worked hard to build over the years. My whole business."

"I've heard a different version of the story," I say.

"What? Who's telling lies?" He looks left and right as though his enemies are right beside him. He shivers and scratches his arms.

"You see, Langa," I say, "you are not in a good place. You fear everything and everybody."

"No, I only fear my enemies." As he speaks, his face looms close to mine, his eyes clouded by tiny red veins. "But the problem is, enemies—they are everywhere."

A thick vein stands out on his temple. His tension is so palpable, I can almost feel the headache myself. I can't help but reach out to touch it, soothing it with my cold fingers.

He steps back, startled. "What did you just do?"

"Tell me the truth," I say. "Who is initiating these hostilities? Is it you or others?"

"I felt that," he insists. "I felt the power leaving your fingers. What did you just do?"

He stares at me and I stare back.

"Who?" I persist. "You or Bo or someone else?"

"Bo," he lies. "I just want to live in peace." He steps back, out of reach, as if anticipating some powerful lightning bolt from my fingertips because of his failure to tell the truth.

I stare at him. "I wouldn't have helped you anyway," I say, "but at least you could respect me enough to tell me the truth. Now go away. I won't ask the ancestors to protect you."

He takes a deep breath. "I'm sorry," he says. "Forgive me. I wasn't lying—I just wasn't telling you everything."

"Sin of omission…" I mutter.

"We are both doing things we shouldn't do. It is out of my control."

"It is within your power to stop this," I say.

We eye each other. He's a brutally powerful man but I can sense how fast his heart is beating. And as much power as he has, he thinks he has to make these choices to keep that power. Which makes him powerless. And afraid. And alone.

"I need your help," he shouts suddenly. "I don't want to die."

"I'm staying away from your dirty taxi war," I snap.

"You're not staying away from this war," he yells. "What about your boyfriend? Did you give him a protective charm?"

I draw in a sharp breath. "Are you threatening him? Because yes, he has the protection of my ancestors and if you even touch—. You don't want to step down that path. Snakes and dogs and my amadlozi guard that way…"

"I won't hurt him," he says. "But I'm asking you for similar help. So that *my* enemies don't harm me."

"No," I say. "You must stop doing what you're doing." I keep my voice low but definitive so he cannot mistake what I am saying. "That is the only way to achieve protection."

"Makhosi," he begs. "Please. I'm afraid."

"You're leading yourself into danger," I say. "If you wish to leave fear behind, then stop the violence."

"And just let the lice eat the hut I've built?"

"It's business," I say. "You don't have to make it a criminal enterprise."

"Please," he begs again. "I need protection."

I shake my head. "You won't get protection, not from me, and not from any sangoma. You are digging your own grave, building your own prison cell."

"Makhosi! No!"

I stare at him. He's a gangster but even a gangster has respect for a sangoma. His eyes drop and he turns away, finally understanding that my "no" is final.

"Langa," I say.

He stops but keeps his back to me.

"Your name means *sun*," I remind him. "You should be true to your name. Why do you seek darkness and violence? You could stop this thing. It doesn't have to continue. You can protect yourself by stopping the violence."

His shoulders slump. "There is no stopping this thing," he whispers. "It's too late. I am a walking dead man."

He gestures and a taxi roars down the road, rattling loud music, zooming to a stop just behind him. He and his tsotsis hop inside.

As they pull away, the younger of the tsotsis stares at me. He holds two fingers to his temple, like a gun, then points it at me.

CHAPTER THIRTEEN

The Fight

We sit in front of the TV for the next couple of hours, watching our favorite soapies. I don't usually let Zi watch so much but I have to admit, I'm not paying attention. My knees shake. I drink a cup of tea to calm myself down and when Zi asks me what Langa wanted, I just say, "Nothing." She gazes at me with her dark eyes, not accusing exactly but informing me that she knows I'm keeping secrets from her.

Zi finally falls asleep in front of the TV and I have to shake her awake and walk her down the hallway to bed.

I get in beside her and let the darkness settle into night. I think about the tsotsi putting his fingers like a gun to his head. Did he mean he was going to come back and try to kill me? Or just that he wishes I was dead?

I wasn't afraid when I said all those things to Langa…but now I am. The courage of the ancestors may be with you at one time but departs you later, when you're just human, 17 years old, a girl, an older sister, waiting to hear from your boyfriend whose life is in danger.

My whole body is aching for Little Man to call now—anger gone, only a trace of fear from Langa's visit left. All fear now concentrated on this man I love. Where is he? Why haven't I heard from him?

In the middle of the night, I'm wakened by the sound of Nhlanhla barking. A jangling sound. Somebody's rattling the gate. I fumble out to the hallway to turn on a light and peek out the front window to see who is there. I can't make out the shadow but Nhlanhla's bark is happy and she's wagging her tail so I open the first door.

"Khosi?" It's Little Man's voice, the sound of it as dear to me as Zi's.

A rush of gladness practically gives me a heart attack. "Little Man!" I rush to unlock the second door and then go to the gate to let him in. His face is hidden behind the bags he's holding. "What time is it?"

"I don't know, two or three in the morning. I brought you something."

In the dark, he hands me a heavy bag and holds onto another one himself. "Groceries?"

"Ehhe," he says.

"Oh, Little Man, thank you!"

"I can't have my girl go hungry." I can *feel* his grin, even though I can't see it in the dark and around the heavy bags. "You need to eat. You must keep that *amazing* body." He inhales and releases his breath in a slow, whistled sigh. "Those sexy curves. They make me think I've died and gone to heaven."

"Little Man," I say. "Stop it!" Even at this hour of the morning, I look left and right to be sure nobody is outside listening.

He reaches over and gently slaps my backside. "Why are you ashamed?" he says. "I'll shout it from the rooftops!" He takes a deep breath and shouts, "I love Khosi Zulu's amazing, sexy bod—"

I clamp my hand over his mouth. "Little Man! You'll wake everybody up."

He grins at me, unrepentant.

I peek inside the grocery bags and shout in delight over the things he brought. "Oranges! Cabbage! Tomatoes! Zi is going to be so excited in the morning."

"I know you like vegetables," he says. "As for me, meat and pap, that's all I need."

"No," I start to argue, "your body *needs* vegetables, unless you want to be getting sick all the time—"

"Eish, Khosi, I was just joking," he interrupts.

My little argument melts away. I don't look at him as I speak. "I was worried about you, Little Man," I say. "Why didn't you answer your phone? Or call me back?"

His arms go around me. "I'll tell you all about it."

His breath is sour. He sways against me.

I step back to glare at him. "Have you been *drinking*?"

"A couple beers, that's all." He holds his hands in the air, the way I've seen other men do—defensive, about ready to fight. As though *I'm* being unreasonable.

"We *discussed* this." All my relief at seeing him is robbed by his breaking of this promise. "I don't care if you drink sometimes, that's not the problem, but I don't want you coming here if you've been drinking. I don't want Zi to see it, to see *you*—drunk."

"S'thandwa," he groans. His fingers clutch my hips, sweet fire spreading to our lips as he pulls me in for a kiss. "I know. *I know*, Khosi. But I just had to see you."

I sigh. My anger burns out quick quick. "Well, come in then. I've been worried all day. I am just glad you're alive."

Inside, I see what was invisible in the dark. "Little Man! What happened to your face? You weren't fighting, were you?"

He touches his swollen eye, the dark skin angry purple and red. "One of Langa's thugs hit me at the taxi rank."

I've been holding my breath. Now I let it out slow, slow, so he can't hear it swoosh out in fear. "You got in a fight?" It could have been worse. He could have been shot.

"Ehhe. Eish, there's already a full-on taxi war. Langa's trying to take over Bo's route."

"I know," I say, deciding to keep silent about Langa's visit—for now. What would Little Man think—or do—if he knew? In any case, other things are more important than that. I ask the most important questions: "What are you going to do? What is Bo going to do?" I feel the power in my fingertips, lightly grazing his skin. I'm begging him with everything in me, *Please say you'll stop working until this has blown over. Please say you won't get involved, that this is not your fight.*

He shrugs and the gesture…it makes my heart drop. Little Man has grown so tall and strong in three years, I forget he's only eighteen. He has a man's job. He has a man's ways. He has a man's way of looking at me. But in that shrug, he seems once again like the young boy I fell in love with. Innocent, vulnerable. Why should he have to shoulder this burden? Here we are, young still but holding the heavy world in our hands.

This isn't what I wanted for you, my heart says.

"Wait here," I tell him.

I run out to the garden to get some dirt. I mix it with water, shibhoshi, and blue spirit to make a quick poultice, which should draw out the heat and swelling. He stays perfectly still while I dab it on the skin swelling around his eye, but I can feel him watching me with his other eye. His hand drops to my waist and he twirls me around, draws me into his lap, arms around my waist, his face buried in the nape of my neck.

"Khosi, please," he whispers.

"What?"

"You know what I want. It's the only thing I want. I'll do—I'll do anything."

Everything in me wants to say yes to his quiet plea. *Yes, Little Man. Come live here. With me.*

Now that the cleansing is over, there's no reason why he couldn't, except for the reason that I promised Gogo. And that's why I can't say yes. So I ignore the question. I don't mean to be cruel. I just don't know what to say.

I've never told him about the promises I made to Gogo—not to become serious with him until I finish school. It seems like a betrayal of her. Would he think she didn't love him? That she didn't want us to be together? Because the truth is, she thought the world of Little Man. She called him grandson, and Gogo didn't do that unless she meant it.

But maybe there is something else holding me back? Is it possible that I'm just using Gogo as an excuse? No. No! I *want* to be together. But I want to know I have Gogo's blessing also.

"Come," I say instead. "Let's get some rest."

We lay down together on the mattress in the living room. I shift on my side and he puts his arms around me from behind, burying his face against my hair.

"I love you, Khosi," he whispers, almost like a prayer, just before drifting off to sleep.

I lay awake for awhile, thinking about everything that's happened in the last day or two. Warning Ahmed. The taxi war. Langa's visit. Little Man. I drift off to sleep, murmuring my own kind of prayer. Gogo, please… I want to be able to say yes…please let me tell Little Man yes.

I wake early, long before first light. I extricate myself from Little Man's embrace and go to the kitchen, light the stove. While the water boils, I pet Nhlanhla absently and stare out the window at my hut in the back—the hut that Gogo and I built before she died so that I could practice as a sangoma. It makes me sad that it hasn't yet been used much. In the moonlight, it casts a shadow into MaDudu's yard.

Ah, yes, MaDudu. From neighbor to enemy to beloved friend. She has turned out to be a true friend and she is forever sorry that she asked that witch to come after us, to come after me, when Mama was still alive because Mama had stolen money from her.

I should ask her what she thinks about all this taxi war business.

When the rooibos tea is ready—extra sweet the way Little Man likes it—I take a cup into the bedroom to rouse him. He can't be here when Zi wakes up: I don't want her to know he spent the night. And besides, I have another long day ahead of me if we're going to walk to her school again, so I have to get her up and out the door.

He wakes slow, one hand stealing out to caress my arm while he takes sips of tea with the other.

"You have to go," I whisper. "I need to get Zi ready for school."

"It's early," he whispers back. "Why are you waking her so early?"

I stare at him. Has he gone mad?

"Khosi," he says. "You're not walking all the way to town again, are you?"

"Of course, you can't think I'd send her on a khumbi today of all days?"

He sets the tea down and speaks in a normal voice. "I would never let anything happen to Zi."

"Shhh," I shush him as Zi shifts and moans, perhaps startled by the sound of his voice.

I beckon him in to the living room and he comes, reluctantly, a fact that makes me want to clobber him with my words. His eyes are bloodshot—how many beers did he really have yesterday? Is he *still* drunk?

"You can't promise that nothing would happen to her," I say. "Anything can happen when there's a taxi war."

"Ngiyazi," he says. Now those bloodshot eyes are staring at me with frustration. "Ngiyazi, anything can happen. And anything can happen when a beautiful young woman and a young girl walk through the streets of Imbali in the dark."

"It may not be safe but it's safer than going for a ride with a bunch of angry men carrying guns, fighting over territory. In fact, why are you even going to work?"

"I can't quit just because of this thing," he says.

"*Why not?* Why can't you just quit?"

"It's my job, Khosi," he says. His voice is suddenly very quiet. "Do you know how hard it is to find a—"

"Well, Zi's not going with you," I declare. "Not until this thing settles—"

"Enough!" he cuts off my announcement. "I'm out of here. Have a *very* nice day! And night! And a nice tomorrow too. And the day after that! See you sometime."

"I'm just trying to protect my little sister," I say. "Why are you getting angry?"

"Because you seem to be forgetting everything about me," he says. "Zi is not just *your* little sister. We've been together so long—she's like my own sister. Do you think I wouldn't do anything to protect her? You and Zi aren't alone. But you would never know it, would you, from the way you're acting."

"But we are alone," I say. "We live here alone."

"Well, you don't have to," he shouts. "You are living here alone because you refuse to live with me. How much longer will you refuse me? Or do you just intend to refuse me forever?"

"Little Man!" I'm aghast.

He drops his face into his hands. "You don't need to worry about this thing anymore, Khosi," he says. "I won't ask again."

"What do you mean?" *Does he mean we're done?* Is he…breaking up with me?

He stands and fumbles at the lock on the door. I bring the keys, start to say, "Little Man," and everything inside me wants to spill out, to tell him that it's not just Zi I'm worried about but I'm worried for him too, and that he *can* quit his job, that it's too dangerous, and that yes, yes, yes, I'll be with him. Especially if he'll quit his job. That we can make this work. That I'll tell Gogo something to keep her quiet, how could she know about this before she died? And besides, I don't think it was Little Man she was opposed to, she just wanted me to finish my schooling before we got serious... So maybe she won't bother me so much if I go back on this promise.

But he doesn't let me say a word. He stops me with a final, cold, "I don't want to hear it, Khosi. I won't hear no from you again."

The door bangs open and he stalks to the gate, which is also locked. "Please," I say, "listen to me," but he turns around and glares at me with so much anger in his eyes that I back away instead. I simply hand him the keys so he can unlock the gate. Nhlanhla dances around us, barking, and Zi comes running to the door in her nightshirt.

"Did you just get here, Little Man?" she calls, running over. "I'm not ready yet. Is the taxi already waiting? It's so early."

He's outside the gate, closing it, and I can see part of him thinks about just taking off. But he stops. He bends down so he's level with her. And his voice is gentle when he speaks to her. "Zi, you and Khosi are going to walk to school again today. I hope things are safer tomorrow. If they are, I'll be here for you. Promise."

She starts to cry. He reaches two fingers through a hole in the fence and she grabs them with her hand.

"Are you going to be OK?" she asks.

"I'll always be OK," he says. "And I will always be here for you. Ngiyathembisa?"

Then he stands, straightens, and brushes the backs of his pants...like he's brushing me off. He doesn't look at me. He doesn't look once before he strides away, up the hill towards his own house.

CHAPTER FOURTEEN

PUTTING ONE FOOT IN FRONT OF THE OTHER

"Don't cry, Khosi," Zi says for the tenth time as we trudge through the dark and the cold, up and down the winding dirt roads of Imbali towards downtown Pietermaritzburg. It's been ten mornings of walking to school in the dark, ten mornings of no Little Man. The lights of downtown twinkle at us through the distance and the world is bathed in pinky-orange light as the morning sun peeks over the Drakensburg Mountains behind us. Despite the beauty of the clear winter morning, I'm crying again. "Little Man said he'll be safe. Don't you believe him?"

"Of course I believe him," I lie. Lying is not something I like to do, not ever, especially not to Zi. But I feel like I've become very good at it since Gogo died. I feel like I'm lying to everybody all the time. Including myself. Ngiyagula, it makes me so sick. I decide to visit Makhosi later. I'll take her a jar of herbs and ask her for a cleansing. And, "We should go to mass this week," I say. "We haven't gone in, oh, a long long time."

We haven't gone since Gogo died. I want to believe God is on my side but he doesn't seem as real to me as amadlozi. I don't hear *his* voice in my head all the time. *He* isn't always telling me do this, do that. In fact, he is always perfectly silent.

"Yebo," Zi says. She reaches out and grabs my hand and gives me a sideways smile. I can always count on Zi to enthusiastically support my ideas. "Let's go. It would make Mama and Gogo happy."

For some reason, the walk seems shorter today. We share a package of biscuits as we walk and arrive in plenty of time for Zi's first class. After brushing crumbs off Zi's uniform, I wave goodbye, calling out "Sharp sharp," and head back to Imbali to see Makhosi, even though I'll need to turn back around to pick Zi up only two or three hours after I get there.

Another day of walking. Sometimes that's all we can do. All the time, worrying if Little Man is safe. Wondering if the fight we had almost two weeks ago is the end of this thing. He wouldn't just end three years of together just like that, would he? It is small comfort that he told Zi he would always be there for *her*. There was a pointed message in that.

Plus, he hasn't called since the fight. We've never gone more than a day or two without speaking before.

So much for promising Zi he would always be there for her.

I try to ignore the ache in my chest. Maybe if I pretend it isn't there, it'll go away.

Even though two clients are waiting on chairs outside her hut, Makhosi calls me in right away. The scent of burning impepho inside her hut is one that fills me with both nostalgia and excitement, the same feeling I get when I use it myself to help a client. And it's true, that's also the feeling I get when I walk inside a school and think about all that I'm going to learn. But I can't think about that. Is it over? All my dreams? School…and Little Man?

We sit down on the goatskin mat in the middle of her hut, her hands gripping mine. Her soft wrinkled flesh reminds me of the way Gogo's hands felt in the last months and weeks of her life, when she really depended on me, when I had to help her do everything.

"What is this thing that is worrying you?" she asks.

I let a big whoosh of air escape my lips. "Everything," I say.

She smiles, pats my knee. "Speak openly. Amadlozi are listening."

I sigh and begin to list all the problems. "I'm not attracting a lot of business yet so I'm not making enough money."

She has a pot of water heating over the fire in the center of the hut. She pours the hot steaming liquid into a cup of herbs and hands it to me to drink.

I put it on the ground before me, to let it cool before I drink it.

"I need to put food on the table and continue to pay Zi's school fees, the ones that are left over after her scholarship," I continue. "Not to mention that I couldn't pay my own fees. Also, the taxi wars are starting again, and Little Man is caught up in the middle of them. I'm worried for his safety." I don't say the thing I'm most afraid of, perhaps even more afraid of than his death: that maybe I pushed him too hard and pushed him away. Forever.

"My aunt and uncle believe I'm a witch. They no longer speak to me."

Her eyes close while I'm speaking. She rocks back and forth, listening. Before long, an almost inaudible hum vibrates through the air.

"And…and…and I think there are people threatening my neighbor, the one who runs the tuck shop a few doors down from my house. I feel like the whole world is conspiring against me…or is evil…or both."

She murmurs, the sound meant to still and soothe me. I try to sit patiently, in silence. But while the outside world may be quiet, the voices inside my head are banging against my brain in a way that is slowly giving me a headache. I lift the cup with its rapidly cooling liquid and take short sips. Makhosi's mixture of herbs has never been my favorite.

"The eye crosses the full river," she says at last. "The eye is always able to do things that the body cannot do. And so the eye is impatient. It wants the body to behave as though it were the eye."

She pauses and is silent for a long time. A low groan breaks the silence.

"You must be patient. All things take time, especially good things. The spirits are on your side. But you must let the river wane. Let the water level fall. Then the body will be able to do what the eye already wants to do. You will cross in good time. Yes, in good time. But the timing will not be of your own making."

Her hand on mine stills the restless spirit inside me. At least, for the moment.

I take a quick detour home to feed Nhlanhla before setting out to fetch Zi. But such a large crowd is gathered on the street in front of the tuck shop and taxi rank that I can barely push through.

My first thought is that something terrible has happened at the tuck shop. After all, MaNene's sons were just threatening Ahmed and his wife not too long ago. But when I reach it, they seem fine. Ahmed is helping lead an elderly gogo towards a chair in the shade, while his wife is popping open a cool drink and giving it to one of their children, a little girl of four or five. The little girl carries the drink carefully over to the old woman and offers it to her. The gogo reaches for her pocket as though she wants to pay but the little girl shakes her head and puts her hands behind her back, refusing to accept payment. Meanwhile, Ahmed has already led another gogo towards the shade while his wife brings a chair.

The rest of the crowd is gathered at the place where my street forms a T intersection, right where the taxis sweep through and stop.

"What's going on, Sisi?" I ask a young woman about my age.

"One taxi opened fire on another and killed two people," she says.

"Who?" I'm already pushing my way forward. "Who is it?"

I'm scared—but at the same time, I feel sure I'd know if Little Man was dead, I'd *know* it. And sure enough, it turns out, I'm right. It isn't Little Man's khumbi—that's the first thing I notice. Somebody has removed the bodies from the taxi and laid them out on the ground alongside the vehicle: a young woman and an elderly man.

I turn away, trying to hide the relief flooding my heart, the joy breaking out in a tiny smile that I can't quite suppress. That it isn't Little Man. At the same time, horror that this is happening.

"Hey! Makhosi!" somebody yells. "Hey! Hey, wena! Makhosi!"

A crowd forms around me quickly, preventing me from leaving. Gently, they push me towards the bodies. I don't bother to resist. The dead can't pay, at least not in money, but you can't deny them their due. This is what I'm here for. Nobody else can do it.

I kneel beside the bodies, a hand on each, and close my eyes. The crowd falls silent, though I can hear their feet shuffling as they watch.

I breathe in deep. The sweat from their bodies and the slightly sour smell of death. The rust scent where the blood seeps out from bullet wounds. The dust from the streets surrounding us and—there it is, the slightest hint of rain in the air. We'll have a thunderstorm tonight. The skies will wash away the blood, attempt to erase the horror from Imbali's streets. But it won't succeed. We are in for it. The wars are only just beginning.

The ancestors hover just behind us, waiting to welcome their two children home. I fumble in my pocket for the bottle of all-purpose muthi I carry with me, a mixture of ocean water, lavender, lemongrass and wild malva, something Mkhulu instructed me to make. In the months since Gogo died, I've discovered it does at least one thing: it calms Zi down instantly, no matter what's happened.

I shake a few drops out onto my index finger, then use it to make the sign of the cross on their foreheads, their mouths, over their hearts. I may be a sangoma, but I'm still Catholic through and through. They need to be welcomed not only by their ancestors but also by the Lord of the Skies.

I open my eyes. Everybody's moved back a few spaces, respectful, but they're all watching. A young girl just three or four years old stands beside her gogo, sucking her thumb. Her gogo is somebody I recognize—Gladys Nene, the woman who ran away from my help when I realized her sons were involved in criminal activities. She's flanked by two stocky young men. In all ways, they look like ordinary men of the township—but I know better. I know they are up to something criminal, even if I don't know the details.

I watch them for a second. She turns slightly and our eyes catch.

She stares hard at me.

I stare back.

She nudges the men and they, too, turn to stare at me. I stare back for some few seconds until I turn away—not because I feel weak or frightened but because the people around us are beginning to notice. Let them think they have the victory. I know the truth.

"Siyabonga, Makhosi," the people murmur as I stumble my way through the crowd. "Thank you, thank you."

At the top of the hill, I see Ahmed and his wife, also watching. They nod respectfully towards me, but I see the doubt in their eyes. They don't know what to think—about me, about my role in the community, about what I just did. I wish I could tell them I welcome their prayers to Allah and I believe the woman and the man who died would now too—even if they wouldn't have before they passed along to the other side.

Walking away, I can't help breathing a sigh of relief. Little Man is still safe. Thank you, Mkhulu, thank you, Gogo.

But then I'm struck by an even more terrible thought than the idea that Little Man could be dead. What if he was part of this? What if Bo and Little Man fired the shots that killed these two people?

The thought makes my face break out in a cold sweat. I grab a fence post to support myself.

First thought: *No. Absolutely not*! Little Man may be working for a taxi involved in this war but he'd never... He'd never! Right, Gogo?

Second thought: *I don't want to think about this anymore*. Because what if I'm wrong? Please, Gogo, don't let me be wrong.

I make my way toward our house, mechanically letting myself inside the gate and making sure Nhlanhla has food and water. Then I head back out for the long walk to pick up Zi.

I'm glad I have something to do, even if it's just putting one foot in front of the other.

CHAPTER FIFTEEN

Under Water

The mother and young child, perhaps two or three years old, lean against my gate, waiting for me as I walk home from dropping Zi at school. I hurry to let them in the gate, shooing Nhlanhla towards the hut and away from them. They follow me inside the yard and I ask them to wait while I drop my bag in the house, then enter the hut to cleanse it with incense and impepho.

They enter and sit near the fire. Nhlanhla lies down patiently near the entrance, her eyes on me. I pat her head, still sweeping impepho through the air. Then at last, I sit. The mother holds her young child in her lap and keeps her eyes down, respectful. The child sits limply and does not move.

"How can I help you, Mama?" I ask. I respectfully avert my eyes from the powerful ancestor that sits just beside her, folding legs exactly the way she does, tilting her head in the same manner. She was an older sister, one that died when this woman was very young, but they had bonded in the way of sisters. And now the older one stays with the younger, to protect and love her.

If I were to die before Zi, that is exactly how I would be. Fierce and protective.

"My child will not eat, Makhosi," she says.

"Have you taken her to the doctors?"

She nods. In that brief movement, I see how tired and worried she is.

"She looks healthy," I say.

"The doctors say she is not thriving," she says. The stark words steal my breath. "She has not grown since her last visit six months ago."

The ancestor sitting beside her jerks her head suddenly. This bothers her badly. She feels every emotion her sister experiences and she is just as tired and worried as the one who still lives.

"Look at her. Her eyes are lifeless." She turns the child around to look at me. The black eyes are like a deep, empty hole.

"I have sought help from other sangomas," the mother says now. "Nothing has helped."

"Did the child eat well before? When she was younger?"

"She ate so much, my husband called her Locust." Even tired as she is, the woman smiles, remembering the nickname. "He joked that she would eat our entire house in days if we let her loose."

"Did she stop eating suddenly, Mama? Or did it happen gradually?"

"No, Ma, I remember exactly when it happened." Her words are eager and sudden. "We had a party and my husband's ex-wife arrived uninvited. She was drunk and caused a big, big scene. Sho! I thought she was going to slap my husband from here into the next world."

"Why was she so angry?"

"Because of the damages," she said.

"What damages? For who?"

"Their daughter had a child before getting married and my husband has not gone to the boyfriend's family seeking damages. The ex-wife is afraid their daughter will never marry now, or fetch a very low lobola because of the child, and that the boyfriend will never help care for the child."

This is exactly the sort of situation that can sour relationships. Sometimes I have had enough thinking about witches. It is a sore subject. But I must ask.

"Do you think she is angry enough to harm your daughter? To put muthi in her path? To have her cursed?"

"Ehhe. I think so, perhaps. It was only after that day, she refused to eat. And she has hardly eaten since. When she tries, she vomits."

"Did you see evidence of muthi?" I ask.

She shakes her head. "Nothing, Makhosi."

I sigh and watch her ancestor, the sister, the one so jealous of her. Jealous in a good way. She wants nothing more than to protect this woman and her daughter. She pleads with me to do something, to find something.

"What are your names?" I ask.

"I am Nobuhle Dube and my daughter is Liyana Ndlovu."

Liyana. It is raining. A name to inspire hope for those whose work is the land, as in the old days, but perhaps a name of sorrow for city dwellers of today.

"How old is Liyana?"

"Four."

Shame, it's not possible. She looks half that age. Two, or even a little younger.

I stoke the fire and let the smoke rise up through the hole in the top. I spread out a bright cloth and throw the bones and items I've collected, to see what they will tell me. Gogo, Mkhulu, help. Help me see what is wrong with Liyana.

I let the amadlozi speak. I cannot lie, it is terrifying what they show me.

I said once that I do not believe in purging for purification. Eish, I would rather do the purging than what they tell me.

Nobuhle's head is bowed as she waits. Liyana has started to droop against her, and she has trouble holding up her neck. I can see more clearly now what I failed to see before. She is wasting away.

"Mama," I say. "MaNdlovu."

She jerks to attention, looking my way.

"Mama," I say. "The amadlozi have told me what to do."

"Is it, Makhosi?"

"Yebo. Kodwa…it scares me."

"Haibo. It scares *you*?"

"It scares me."

She takes a deep breath. "Tell me."

"They say to put her under the water. She must learn to breathe under water. And then she will be cleansed."

Nobuhle scrambles to her feet, clutching her daughter close. I stand too, quick quick. Her ancestor jumps up, steadies the woman with her arm. She breathes in deep, her chest heaving.

Nobuhle's dead sister rubs her arm gently. Though Nobuhle doesn't feel the soft touch in her body, she senses it in her spirit. Slowly, the grey look of her skin returns to normal. Tears trickle down her cheeks. "What you are asking is too terrible, Makhosi," she says.

"Ngiyaqonda." I understand, I do. It is too much. It is terrible. I think back to my own experience learning this, the panic, the letting go, the push and pull, between the amadlozi and my breathing and the watery depths. It was so hard, how could I possibly ask another person to do it? But it is not me saying this, asking this.

"You have a powerful ancestor who mirrors you in every step," I say. "I do not think she wants harm to come to your child. And…I do not want it either. Liyana will be safe. With everything that I can possibly promise, I will keep her safe. I will go under water with her. I will not leave her there."

Her arms close protectively around Liyana. She closes her eyes, buries her nose in her child's neck, smells her skin.

I wonder what it is like to love somebody that much? It is hard to imagine. Did Mama love us that much? If so, why didn't she do what she needed to get medicine for her HIV so she could live? Fear is crippling. Gogo, may I never be so afraid that fear wins.

"Mama, can we?" I ask.

Nobuhle breathes out slow. Then, even slower, she hands Liyana over to me.

Her body is so frail, so light. It feels like I'm holding a small bundle of kindling sticks.

"Woza," I say and Nobuhle follows me out of the hut and into the house. We go inside and to the bathroom, where I begin to fill the bathtub with warm water, letting it fill as deep as possible. Directing Nobuhle to sit on the toilet and holding Liyana with one hand, I take my skirt off with the other. Then I get in.

Mkhulu, are you sure about this? Because I am afraid.

I hold Liyana away from me and look at her dull eyes. Then at

Nobuhle. She grips the edge of the toilet as if it is taking everything she has not to snatch her child away.

"No harm will come to her," I promise again, hoping I am telling the truth.

And then I let go and slip under, taking the baby with me.

It is just bath water. Ordinary. It is not a lake, or a river, a reservoir or the ocean. It is clear, not murky, and so easy to emerge from the water again, which is only as deep as the tub. There is nothing dangerous here…no, I am the only danger, the fact that I am holding Liyana under.

What if I drown her? What if I misheard Mkhulu and she dies?

But still, we stay under the water. I hold Liyana still, though truly, she is not struggling. I hold for a count of ten. Twenty. Kunye. Kubili. Kutathu. Kune. Kuhlanu…

And then we come up. Nobuhle is crying, a long low wailing sound, and she does not watch, her head is turned to the wall. Her sister holds her and watches me. Nods briefly as if to say, Kulungile, it is all-right. Keep going. Futhi.

Liyana does not cry. She simply stares at me, unblinking, water dripping off her hair and running in rivulets down her tiny, elfin face. And she is still alive.

"Futhi," I say, and we go under again.

This time, she opens her mouth under water and I think she might start gurgling or choking but she doesn't, she breathes out.

This time, I count to twenty, thirty, forty. And then we come up.

Nobuhle is openly sobbing, hitting the wall with her hand, so hard I am afraid she will make a hole.

"Futhi," I say, and Liyana and I go under again, for a count of thirty and then forty and then fifty. Then sixty. And still we wait.

Liyana's eyes are open and she is watching me. Is it my imagination or does she feel slightly weightier?

I feel the sense of something giving, something going away, something slipping off Liyana and away, into the water. I breathe in and out—yes, under water, but that is the gift the ancestors gave me, and

Liyana shudders, takes her own breath even under water, and everything is calm. And she is distinctly heavier, as though she has taken heft again. As though she is real, and here.

We emerge and I can see now that whatever had hold of her is gone. She shivers in the cold air.

"Mama," I say. "Let us see if she will eat."

Nobuhle snatches her from my arms and smothers her to her chest. Liyana flails and struggles away. She opens her mouth in a long, low wail. But thank you, God, when we take her to the kitchen and offer her some Marie biscuits and rooibos, she eats and slurps the sugary milky tea, eager. Nobuhle stares in amazement, first at her daughter and then at me.

"Eh!" she cries. "How did you do it?" Her eyes alight, eager. This is why I'm a healer, to help people like this.

"It was not me, Mama," I say. "It was your sister, the one who died when you were so young. Do you remember her? She has never forgotten you. She is watching over Liyana and you. And she helped remove this thing that was keeping Liyana from growing. It will be all-right now. Everything will be all-right."

CHAPTER SIXTEEN

INTRUDER

It's late. Zi and I are watching television. The gate rattles and Nhlanhla starts barking fiercely. She knows Little Man's footsteps, knows his scent.

So it's not Little Man then.

I pull the curtain back. I don't recognize the dark shape standing at the gate. It's not my uncle, or any of the neighbors. I let the curtain fall in place. What should I do?

I sit back on the mattress and wait. Zi huddles beside me, looking up at me with her large dark eyes, as if to ask, "Why don't you do something?"

Whoever it is keeps rattling the gate. I don't dare open the door and call out to find out who it is. It's true that neighbors know we live here alone, except for the weekends my uncle comes, but what if it's not a neighbor? I'm certainly not going to let a stranger know that two young girls are here alone late at night.

We sit in the dark. The rattling stops. I sink back into the mattress.

And then Nhlanhla begins to growl, low in the throat. The hair on the ridge of her back sticks straight up.

Zi grabs my arm. I sit bolt upright.

"Khosi," she whimpers but I hush her with a harsh, "Shhhhhhhush."

Footsteps crunch the gravel just outside the door. How in the world did somebody get *inside* the gate? I keep it locked at all times and, like many homes in Imbali, we have barbed wire running the length of the fence.

The sound of footsteps retreats, then returns, closer, closer, right up to the window.

What is he doing? Is he looking through the crack in the curtain? Is he checking the bars across the windows to see if he could somehow break in?

We crouch down against the wall so he can't see our heads in the flickering light of the television. Of course, he must know we're here. Why else is the television on? And lights in the kitchen?

Nhlanhla continues to growl, first at the front door, then she runs through the living room and into the kitchen and growls at the back door.

Why didn't I accept the gun Little Man tried to give me? No, I said, no no no, the Lord in the Sky and the ancestors will protect us. No no no.

Stupid stupid stupid. I would give anything for that gun now. I would give anything for Little Man. Why didn't I say yes, yes, yes, move in, move in now, as soon as Gogo died and he asked if we could live together?

We sit silently, gripping each other. Nhlanhla paces back and forth between kitchen and living room and then down the hallway towards the back bedroom. She lets out a series of sharp, staccato barks.

And then she's silent.

So are the two of us, sitting perfectly still. Everything is still.

"Why isn't she coming back to the living room?" Zi whispers.

I'm too frightened to answer. I know one thing, I'm not going to the back to check. I'll stay right here all night long if I have to.

After some time, Nhlanhla pads back into the living room. She goes to her blanket in the corner. Circles once, twice, three times, then plops down with a long, deep sigh.

Does that mean everything is back to normal? Maybe. But still we don't move.

We must fall asleep because I wake some time later, cramped and cold, my neck aching, Zi curled up right on top of me. The air is frigid. I shove Zi off and run to the bathroom just in time to throw up all over the floor.

I crawl on hands and knees back to the living room.

Zi's already back to sleep. I cuddle up beside her, too sick to clean up after myself or to check the yard to see if our intruder is gone.

We wake in the morning to loud noises, a babbling crowd just outside our gate. I brush my hand across my mouth, which still tastes of puke, wiping off the crusty drool that dried on my cheek.

"Get up, Zi," I say. "Something is happening outside."

"Is it?" She yawns and stretches.

My bones ache from our awkward sleep. But at least we made it through the night. Nobody broke in. Nobody killed us. Nhlanhla is standing at the door, whining to be let out, and as soon as I open the door, she bounds out the door and runs to the gate, barking at the people shoving and pushing to be in front.

I walk towards the yelling crowd. The gate is closed and I assume the lock is still on it—whoever was in our yard last night must have climbed over the barbed wire that surrounds the yard.

And then I see it.

"Zi, get back inside," I say quick quick.

"What? Why?" And then she sees it too because she screams.

"Get back inside," I shout. "Hamba!"

She twirls around and runs back to the house, slamming the door behind her.

I advance more slowly. My focus narrows in on the body of the man slumped against the gate.

"Who is it?" I call.

Several people in the crowd look east, towards the tuck shop at the top of the hill. The tuck shop is burning, flames leaping high in the early morning sky. And the person slumped against my gate is Ahmed. I don't even have to feel him to know his body is cold. His spirit left hours ago.

The people gathered around him look somber, but up the hill young men toyi-toyi in front of the shop as it burns.

I don't even think. I jerk open the gate. The lock is broken. Ahmed's body slumps back into the yard. I shove his body into my yard and pull the gate shut. Then I glare at the crowd before stalking up the hill.

"What do you have to say for yourself?" I scream at the young men. Who are they? They are just showing their faces to God and everybody, no fear. Don't they understand we could identify them later to the police? That they could end up in jail? "You are terrible. Terrible, terrible men!" I yell.

They stop their dance and surround me, I suppose in an attempt to intimidate me, their lips grinning, deep growls in their throats. They toyi toyi. But they can't make me fear them. Maybe if Zi was here, that would work. I would always be afraid for her and need to protect her.

"Go home," I shout. "Be terrible there. I for one don't want you anywhere near my street. Get out of here. Hambani! Hambani!"

They disperse slowly, just as the sound of sirens breaks over the hill that separates Pietermaritzburg from Imbali. A fire engine chugs up the main street, and then up the dirt road toward the smoke.

Nobody's standing here watching. They've all gone home. I suppose my yelling shamed them…or something. Perhaps they simply don't want to face the police.

And then I remember. I told MaNene that I would offer Ahmed protection. I told her that I would pray for him. That I wouldn't let her sons harm him. Perhaps she told her sons what I had said. Did they do this? Did they kill Ahmed and leave him at my gate? If so, what message are they sending me? Are they challenging me? Are they challenging the power of Mkhulu? And who were those young men dancing in the street in front of the tuck shop, as if they had nothing to fear?

And if it's not MaNene's sons, who is it, and what is the warning I'm supposed to understand from this?

I walk back home, wondering what I've stopped. Or what I may have started.

CHAPTER SEVENTEEN

SIFISO

I keep Zi home that day, worried about what might happen if we leave the house unprotected. Careful, we watch the smoking remains of the tuck shop, and the curious people who wander by to see what happened. I circle the yard several times slowly, looking for signs of muthi—white powder or a mud mark on the house. It is not that I think we have been cursed but only that I cannot imagine any other reason why whoever did this to Ahmed would leave his body at my house. They wish to discredit me. They wish to say to the neighbors, *See? See? She is not this great thing, the sangoma who can help you. She is just a girl and she has no power. In fact, do with her as you wish.*

Though it takes them some time to show up, two police officers finally arrive to remove Ahmed's body. I ask Zi to wait inside while I speak to them. She holds the thick brown curtains to the side and watches us, scrunching her nose against the window, making funny faces at the officers.

The younger officer introduces himself as Sifiso. He is short with a compact, muscular body. He has a very wide smile and very white teeth. Nobody would call him handsome but there's something about his face I really like, open, a lightness, sunshine. "Your little sister is cute," he says. "She reminds me of my niece."

"Thanks," I say, feeling a puff of pride, as though I'm somehow responsible for her sparkling personality, the way she catches people's attention, or her beauty.

"We are sorry for the intrusion," he says, "but we must ask some few questions."

He isn't much older than me, maybe twenty years old? As he talks, he keeps looking at me, that wide mouth constantly smiling. He's working hard, trying to put me at ease. Even though he's young, wrinkles around his kind brown eyes suggest that he is a man with much laughter in him. He's an interesting contrast to the other police officer, who also looks kind but older and tired somehow.

I shrug. "That's fine. I'll answer any questions."

"What was your relationship to the deceased?" he asks.

"He owned the tuck shop at the top of the hill. I saw him every day." I point to the thin trail of grey smoke where the tuck shop is burning and shake my head. "We spoke in passing, that is all."

Sifiso nods at me, his eyes grave.

"You have no idea why somebody would kill him?" the older officer asks.

"People seemed angry that a Somali owned the tuck shop," I say. "It used to be owned by a man who grew up in the neighborhood. He lived in the house next door, behind the shop. But Ahmed lived somewhere else with his wife and children. Perhaps he didn't feel safe."

"Why would neighbors be angry?" Sifiso asks.

He shifts so that he's just that much closer to me. A centimeter, maybe half a centimeter, but I notice.

I move back a step. He moves in to fill the open space between us. Something connects us, I can feel it, this heat, this strong pull between us.

And I like it.

I like the way he stands too close. I know, without having to ask, that he doesn't question all eyewitnesses this way. I want him to stand even closer. Then I think of Little Man and shake that thought from my head.

"Have the neighbors made comments that would indicate they are angry?" he prompts.

He rests an arm on the fence and now his arm is touching mine, just barely. My arm hairs spring to alertness, aware of his skin gently touching mine.

Did he do that on purpose, Gogo, or was it an accident?

I don't move my arm. I don't move to create distance between us. I leave it just as it is, keeping my eyes on his. If he takes his arm away, I'll know he's touching me on accident.

He doesn't take it away.

Our arms rub gently against each other.

"It is the same as in other places," I say. "They were not really angry at Ahmed."

"You knew his name?" the older officer asks.

For some few seconds, I'd forgotten he was even there. I veer my gaze towards him. "He may not have lived here in Imbali but he owns the tuck shop. So he was my neighbor," I say. "I know all my neighbors' names."

He makes note of this while Sifiso prompts me again. "So your neighbors are not angry at Ahmed in particular. Why are they angry?"

"They are angry that they don't have jobs, that they have no money. They are angry that this man is from somewhere else, not even South Africa, and yet he has a business and he makes a lot of money from us..." I stop. The two men are watching me carefully. I sigh. "Sorry," I say. "I'm only repeating what they have said or what I feel,"—I take a leap of faith and say it—"what I feel the ancestors have told me when I have been consulting with clients."

"You are a sangoma?" Sifiso asks.

I nod, heart warming to the way respect suddenly deepens in his voice. His arm moves ever so slightly, sweet sweet, his skin feeling like the softest of caresses against mine.

"Can you think of a reason why the man was killed in front of your house?" he asks.

I shake my head, but if it was deliberate, if it was retribution, those people will pay for it. The wrath of the ancestors is no joke, and nothing is hidden from them, nothing.

But this I cannot say out loud because I do not know anything for certain. And Zulus, we don't whisper. Whispering is the supreme rudeness. But also, it is dangerous. Because you might be whispering harmful secrets about your neighbors or family members or friends. And so likewise, I will say nothing out loud that I do not know to be true.

"I don't know why," I say, "but somebody entered my yard last night. They crept around in the dark. My dog was inside but she was barking at them and they left. It scared me."

"Do you live here alone?" the older officer asks.

"With my little sister," I say. "My uncle used to come visit on the weekends…" I stop because what can I say about the family situation? It is too much painful to share with strangers.

The older officer shakes his head. "You shouldn't live here alone. It isn't safe."

"What am I supposed to do?" I ask. "If you have a solution for me that doesn't involve living with strangers, I will listen."

Sifiso stares at me. "You are a brave woman, Makhosi," he says. Our arms are still touching. Gently, his finger rubs against my arm. His hand trembles a little when he touches me and suddenly, I can barely breathe.

I hiccup. Glance from where his hand is touching me to his eyes. I can't look away. I mean that. I can't—or perhaps it is just that I don't—look away.

More police arrive and then an ambulance, parking on the edge of the street where it's crumbling into a small, unofficial channel for water runoff, the EMT crew climbing out of the cab and circling around the body. I retreat to the porch and Zi joins me. The police cordon off a large square area that extends from the street to our yard. A white man in a tan suit parks just outside our gate in a little Golf Citi. He gets out and speaks with Sifiso and his partner. Sifiso gives me a chin nod and then the two of them walk away and start speaking to the neighbors still clustered in small groups and watching the police activity warily. As my neighbors speak with them, some reluctantly, some eagerly, they ask questions and take notes. A long time later, when they've disappeared from sight, a police photographer arrives and starts taking meticulous photos of the scene from every possible angle.

I hope this means that Ahmed will receive justice.

A reporter arrives and starts filming until the white man speaks to him, gesticulating with his hands and pointing, and then the reporter retreats to the tuck shop and begins taking photos of that instead. Before long, he's interviewing neighbors. I decide this would be a propitious time to retreat—I have no interest in appearing in this news story as the wild-eyed sangoma who lives in the house just where a Somali man was murdered. *That* sounds like a really great way to kill my business before it has a chance to even become something.

I check my cell phone. Nothing from Little Man. All these long weeks and still he maintains silence. Maybe that fight really was the end after all.

I scan the street to see if Sifiso has returned, but I see no sign of him. My whole body feels hollow with desolation, as though I've been abandoned, which is ridiculous, honestly. I just met him. And I have a boyfriend—a boyfriend who isn't speaking to me right now, apparently, but still, a boyfriend. Is it, Gogo? Maybe I feel abandoned by Little Man, not Sifiso. So why is Sifiso the one I am thinking of?

"Zi, we're going to clean the house," I say.

"Aw, Khosi, do we have to?" she groans.

I hand her the broom. "Start in the bedroom," I say. "I'll start in the bathroom."

"It *stinks* in there. Why did you throw up, Khosi?"

"I fell sick," I say.

Maybe cleaning house will help me forget what's going on.

After I finish the bathroom, I fill a bucket with fresh water and soap and a few rags, and go after the windows. I wash and dry every corner of every window, glancing out the window every few seconds to see if Sifiso returns. Why am I so concerned about where he is and when he'll return? I have no right to these feelings. In fact, they're a betrayal of everything I do have with Little Man.

When the windows can't be cleaned any more, I attack the cupboards in the kitchen, mostly empty after Auntie cleaned it out. I wash the cracked tabletop. I dust the television carefully, and even get behind it, where I find evidence of a mouse. Nhlanhla pushes up behind me, her wet nose chilling the backs of my knees, squeezes around me and goes crazy sniffing the mouse hole.

"Nhlanhla," I scold. "You're supposed to take care of these mice for me. You're not here for protection only, you know. You must earn your keep."

I know, not all dogs kill mice, but Nhlanhla is that kind of dog known for catching rats and mice. She slinks to the corner, ashamed by the scolding.

We're all startled by a knock on the door. Nhlanhla breaks into a series of shrill barks. A sudden sweet thrill rips through my stomach. Cleaning the house did the trick, apparently, and helped me forget everything happening in the front yard. But my body remembered all the time.

I throw the front door open. I know I must have the most foolish grin on my face. Sifiso stands there, holding out three ice-cold bottles of Coke, returning my welcoming face with his own broad smile. He reaches out to pat Nhlanhla on the head, scratching her under the chin. "Join me on the porch for cool drinks," he invites. "And I'd like to meet this little sister of yours."

We sit on the cement floor of the porch, our backs against the house wall—Zi, me, and then Sifiso. Sifiso sits just close enough that our legs brush up against each other, barely touching but enough that I'm aware of it. I glance sideways, only to find his eyes on me. I shift, disconcerted.

"So you make a living as a sangoma?" he asks.

Zi bursts out giggling. I glare at her and then say, "I'm just starting out. I try but it's been difficult."

"Why?" he asks.

From the way he watches me intently and waits for my answer, I can tell he genuinely wants to know.

"I grew up here, in this very house," I say. "Everybody still thinks of me as a little girl. It's hard for them to see me as a sangoma."

"Why don't you move somewhere else?" He gestures at my place with his hand. "You are all alone, you and your sister. What is keeping you here?"

Zi leans in to look up at my face. She is wondering the same thing. *Please don't mention Little Man, Zi. Because he is not the reason.*

And I tell him. I tell him something I have never dared tell Little Man. "I want to leave," I say. Zi's mouth parts in surprise. She looks as though she is going to respond, but I rush on with my words to silence her. "I want to start over somewhere—not far, probably Durban. I want to be close to the water. But so far, the ancestors have told me no, don't leave yet, there is still something here for me. But I don't know what that thing is."

Sifiso leans back against the wall as if he's relaxing for the first time since the conversation began. "That makes me happy," he says. "It makes me happy that you are here, now, in this place."

His hand inches towards mine until his pinky finger is hooking around mine, our hands hidden from Zi's view. And now there is no doubt about it, no mistaking Sifiso's intentions. I keep my pinky curled around his. I don't know why. OK, that is a lie, I do know why. I know exactly why. I want to touch him more than that. I want to touch him—oh, all over, I want—

"Or I never would have met you," he whispers. "And I'm really glad I met you."

Later. Later, I will have to think about why my heart responds so quickly to him in this way. Am I that easily swayed from my course? Am I a basically unfaithful person? Later, I will have to think about Little Man and Sifiso and question who I am. But for now…for now gladness shines out of my eyes right back at him.

"I may leave someday," I admit, wanting to be fully truthful. "I don't think they are telling me to stay forever."

"That's OK," he says. "Now that I've met you, wena, that's OK. Even if they tell you to move. Everything else can be planned for now that we know each other."

I have known him some few hours, that is all. Yet it feels like something just became settled between us. Something big.

CHAPTER EIGHTEEN

Thunderstorm

The next day is Saturday so Zi and I don't have to worry about the trip to school. Instead, I hang my sign out, and keep the gate open, waiting for customers. I wait all day and nobody shows up. Not a single soul. Not even Little Man, who usually drops by on Saturdays after his shift is over.

This is the third Saturday since our fight and we haven't seen him once.

After all that gladness and joy of yesterday and Sifiso and the strange happiness in all of that, my whole day is tinged with a strong homesickness for Little Man. I wish he'd just call. Maybe it would help—clear out all these feelings for Sifiso. Make me remember what I'm supposed to be doing. Or who I'm supposed to be loving.

A massive thunderstorm clouds the early afternoon, lightning streaking across the sky, huge drops of water—as big as Zi's hand—smacking the ground, trash and mud spattering down the sides of the street.

At about three in the afternoon, I go to text Little Man when my cell phone rings. I jump to answer it but the caller ID is blocked.

I answer anyway. Maybe it could be somebody calling to tell me something terrible has happened to Little Man. Maybe—and yes, my heart tears open with joy just a little bit when I hear his voice, Sifiso's voice, on the other side.

"May I come by this evening?" He sounds so easy about it all.

I gasp, my breath coming in quick spurts. "Of course," I say. Breathe. "Of course."

"My shift is over at 5," he says. "I'll bring take-out for you and the other little beauty in your household. Do you like Indian?"

I nod, then realize he can't see me. "Yes," I say. "Spicy."

"Truly spicy?"

"As spicy as they can make it."

He chuckles. "I knew from the moment I saw you that there was something I liked about you. I'll just add this to the growing list."

Zi's watching me when I hang up, all smiles. "Who was that?" she asks, mouth pursed in suspicion.

"Sifiso," I say. "He's coming over. He's bringing food."

"What about Little Man?" she asks.

For just a minute, I worry. What if Little Man shows up out of the blue? After all, he used to do that all the time, and why wouldn't he? Especially now, after our fight, he might show up suddenly so we can fix things between us.

"Oh, this isn't like that," I lie. And then wonder who I'm lying to.

A few months ago, a group of amaShembe believers created a large circle of white stones on the empty lot next door to the Dudus house so they can worship there on Saturdays. The Shembe have strange ways, with the Vaseline their prophet blesses and their vuvuzelas instead of church music, but I know the ancestors work with them. I don't mind them, unlike some of the neighbors who do.

Sifiso arrives just as they start their church service, the loud atonal music drifting into our yard, the men's voices rising in a chant and the women responding. Lucky for them, the rain has stopped—but I know from experience that they would have a service, rain or no rain. They are faithful each and every week.

"You have a colorful neighborhood, Khosi," Sifiso says as I open the gate to let him in. He's carrying a large brown paper bag, steam rising from it. That must be the food. He pauses for a second and rustles around in his pocket, then produces a heavy lock with a bolt that could never be cut with simple wire cutters. "I brought you a new lock—hopefully, a better one. It terrifies me to think of you and Zi alone in the house if this person who killed Ahmed comes back."

"Thank you," I say.

"I want to be sure you're safe," he says. "Your neighborhood is both colorful and…it seems…a bit on the dangerous side."

"We have a dog," I remind him.

"Thank God."

"Where did you grow up?" I ask. "Isn't your neighborhood colorful?"

"I grew up right here in Imbali, on Mlahlankosi Road," he says.

"Oh, just the other side," I say.

"Yes. My mother still lives there but I bought a house closer to the city center. I thought it would be interesting to live there."

"Is it?"

We've reached the porch and I notice how carefully he wipes his boots to make sure he doesn't track mud into the house.

"It's like being Catholic, everybody's there, all kinds of people," he says. "There are whites, Indians, coloreds. A Somali family, just like your tuck shop man. We look out for each other. We have neighborhood braais a few times a year. It makes me proud of being South African, not like what you read in the papers. Not like what happened here. We're doing it right that side, the way it should be. A real rainbow nation."

I'm standing at the door, pausing before I open it and invite Zi to join us in this conversation. He moves close so he's standing right next to me. He's much taller but he stands so that we're touching as he looks down at me. I shiver.

"You like reading the newspapers?" I manage to ask.

"I like to keep up with things." His hand brushes against my cheek.

A thunderstorm cracks open the sky shortly after Sifiso arrives. The rain comes in long, staggered downpours, letting up for a few seconds and then starting up again, like an engine stuttering.

We switch the TV off and cover mirrors with cloths and try not to think about the lightning. One time, when my mama was still alive, I actually saw a lightning bird and knew we had been cursed. But that was a long time ago.

We sit on the floor, on the mattress. Zi puts her head in my lap. Sifiso slips his arm behind me, his fingers gently gripping my hip.

"Are you Catholic?" I ask. Voice just a little unsteady. Trying to keep the conversation normal.

"Yebo. Born and baptized," he says. "My job keeps me from going to mass every week but I try to go two or three times a month."

"We used to go every week," Zi says. "But Khosi is not as faithful as Gogo. Or Mama."

I sigh. "I'm sorry, Zi, sometimes I struggle with this thing of God." I look at Sifiso, apologetic. Will he think less of me if I tell the truth? But his hand is a steady pressure on my back. "I want to believe but he doesn't seem as real as the amadlozi. And he left us all alone. Why are we here, without a mother or father or grandmother to help us? Sometimes it makes me angry."

"I struggle too," he reassures me. He reaches his fingers up to thread through my weave. His touch is gentle and loving. I look in his eyes and see nothing but kindness. "I go because it helps me. In this job, it is tempting to accept bribes, but I know I cannot do that if I'm going to church and proclaiming my innocence and honesty before God and everybody. So I must keep going. That is all. Perhaps in the end, you will find it helpful, but you are in this long stretch of deciding what you need. We all have those times in our lives."

I like the way he says this. It makes me think maybe he is right. Maybe I will come through this time of anger and find God on the other side of it, the way I decided I would forgive Mama for the things she did, even though she did not live long enough to make it right.

Zi likes Sifiso, she can't help it, even though her eyes accuse me when he leaves. But all night long, the two of them giggle and laugh while we eat. She likes the way Sifiso bursts into song whenever he feels like it. She likes the way he listens to her when she tells him about school. She likes the fact that he brings her an enormous slice of chocolate cake with about two inches of frosting on it. He brings it out with a flourish and sets it on the kitchen counter. "Phansi, Nhlanhla," he commands and Nhlanhla stops jumping up on the counter.

"But you didn't bring ikhekhe for Khosi," Zi protests.

"Ah, wena, a loyal sister," Sifiso says. "Good girl." Then he pulls a bouquet of delicate orange and white flowers out of the bag and Zi squeals. "I thought instead of cake, I would bring flowers for the lovely sangoma who lives in Imbali, the township named flower." His fingers touch mine as he hands me the freshly cut flowers and my hand trembles.

"Where did you find these, Sifiso?" I ask. These are rare flowers, not the kind I see in the market among the women selling such things.

"I grew them," he says, simply.

"Oh, you like to garden?"

"Everything," he says. "Herbs, flowers, vegetables. African plants. Indigenous plants only. That's very important to me. My back yard is wild with them."

"Can I come see?" I ask.

He nods. "Anytime, Ntombi, you are always welcome in my home. I would love to show you my garden. Perhaps some of my plants will be useful to you."

The words catch in my throat. I want to ask when. I want to ask where. I cannot. But I wish to go now, to see it now now.

"Are you married?" Zi demands.

"No, thando," he tells her. "I live alone. My family visits a lot. It is a small house"—he pauses—"but it is big enough for more than me."

I try not to think about the implications of his statement. "How old are you?" I ask. I had thought he was young but he owns his own house? Of course, I also own my own house.

"Twenty-five," he says. "How old are you?"

"Seventeen," I say. "Eighteen next month."

He whistles. "Seventeen and already in possession of your own house and your own business? You are ahead, Ntombi, ahead of the game. You will see."

"I told you," Zi says. "You're smart enough to go back to school and work. We will figure it out. I'll help you. I'll be the sangoma's assistant."

Sifiso watches me.

"What do you think?" I ask.

"I think you have a great spirit," he says. "It is wide like the ocean. And powerful too, like water. I think you can do whatever you wish to do."

Zi takes her cake into the living room to watch television. I take the opportunity to ask Sifiso about himself.

"Why did you become a police officer?" I ask. "You like to read, you like to garden. You seem—different."

"I wanted to go to school," he says. "I was planning to study medicine or perhaps ecology. It wasn't really possible when I first graduated. My father died ten years ago and my mother needed me to help her. But I don't believe it's ever too late. If something stops you at one time, maybe a door will open up later. Perhaps it looks different than what you planned but if you walk through those open doors, everything becomes bright and possible again, just in a different way. Don't you think?"

"I want to believe that," I say. "I really do. I had to quit school after my grandmother died. And there is nothing I want more than to go to school."

He takes my elbow in his hand. "Oh, Khosi," he says. "That's terrible."

I shake my head and keep my eyes on the cracked cement floor. It's my private shame—not only that I quit school but that when I did, I broke a promise to Gogo.

Sifiso puts his hand under my chin and raises my face until my eyes meet his. He places the palm of his hand on my cheek, then on the back of my head. His fingers tickle the skin on the nape of my neck.

I choke a little, tears stinging the edges of my eyes. "I promised Gogo I wouldn't quit," I say. "I promised her, when she was dying. She—she asked for just two things. She said no matter what, I had to go to school. So I said yes because I've always wanted—I wanted to go to university. But I couldn't pay all the fees." This is the second thing I'm telling Sifiso that I've never told Little Man. But why haven't I told him? Do I think Little Man wouldn't understand or sympathize? After all, look at what *he* gave up. For me.

His grip on my elbow tightens. "What about your relatives? Couldn't they help? Your father?"

A burst of noise from the television gives me time to think about what I should say.

"Baba has never been much help." It sounds blunt when I say it like that but somehow I want Sifiso to know the truth. "He hasn't been part of our lives, not since Zi was very small. I'm not going to ask him for help now, even if he could give it, which I am not sure he could. I do have an aunt and uncle but they both have children of their own and—"

"You and Zi are too much a burden?"

I have no reason to tell him the truth but I do. "They think I used witchcraft to kill Gogo," I say, "after I also used witchcraft to get her to create a will so that the house would come to me after she died."

"I see," he says. And I know, he really does see. "And did you?"

I can't take offense because I know he isn't really asking. So he doesn't wait for me to answer.

"What was the other thing your gogo asked you to promise?" he asks soft soft.

I shake my head. I'm not ready to tell him that yet. How I broke *that* promise too. That is a much bigger conversation, one I haven't had with— well, not with anyone.

He lets it go quickly. "I've only known you one day, Ntombi, but I am certain of one thing already," he says. "This is not the end for you. If you really want to go back to school...you will find a way."

I walk Sifiso to the gate later, much later, when it stops raining. The lights of Imbali twinkle all around us. We avoid puddles and stop at the gate to linger. Neither of us wants this night to end. I'm a little afraid what it will mean when I have to really think about what I'm doing.

"May I come again?" he asks.

I look at the ground and nod. I try not to think about Little Man.

"Then I will return," he says. "Soon."

"I'll expect you," I say. My voice is all wobbly, doing ridiculous things. It even sounds uneven. Giddy and afraid and hopeful, all at once.

A simple soft breath. "It's a promise then."

"Were you worried I would say no?" I ask, glancing up now to see his face. Afraid. What if I see triumph there? As though he already assumes I belong to him and I find I've walked into a trap. But no. The only thing I see is his wide, hopeful smile.

"A little bit," he says. "I felt from the moment I first saw you that somehow we belong together. But that doesn't mean you feel the same way. I don't really know anything about you. Maybe there are things—or people—in your life, another man…?"

"Sifiso, I—"

I stop. I can't answer the last question and I can't say what I want to say, I can't, not yet, if ever. But oh, I *want* to say it. How I feel too. How I also feel like we belong. Even if that's ridiculous. Little Man is who I belong with. Right?

I put my hand on his chin. It feels firm, real. There. Here.

He covers my fingers with his. With his other hand, gentle around my waist, he draws me in close.

His lips are warm and sweet and he tastes a little bit like the cake he brought for Zi, which she shared with him. Sweet and somehow just right. And I kiss him back. Pressing my lips against his, a promise.

He sighs into my mouth. His teeth are soft as he gently bites my cheek and then my ear and then my neck.

"Khosi," he whispers. Squeezes my hand, and is gone.

CHAPTER NINETEEN

Jesus on my Tongue

A thousand worries attack me that night. I lie beside Zi, dreamless, sleepless. Nhlanhla must sense my anxiety. Every so often, she whines in her corner as if to say, "I'm right here with you. I'll stay awake as long as you do."

I must check my cell phone a million times to see if Little Man—or Sifiso—has texted or called.

OK, let's be honest. It is Sifiso whose name I am looking for on the screen.

I think about Little Man and the secret I've been keeping from him. It's not a secret I can keep much longer, though if Little Man has walked out of my life, I must think about how to handle it.

If the truth will come to light no matter what I might want to do to stop it, I must tell Sifiso too. He needs to know. How is he going to react? He may think we belong together now but will he still feel that way when I tell him?

I can't lie to myself, I—I want him. I *want* him. Is he as wonderful as he seems or am I falling for somebody like Thandi's Honest—married with several girlfriends on the side? Thandi fell pregnant when we were just 14 and for awhile she was afraid she might be infected with the disease of the day, HIV. He used her, even beating her up when she confronted him about her situation. They may have gotten back together for a short time but then he moved on. These sugar daddies, they aren't worth it because then you're left with what what—a disease and a baby and who knows what else.

And then there's this other thing: the confidence that both Zi and Sifiso expressed in my ability to somehow find a way to go back to school. The truth is, it seems beyond me. I just don't see how to make it all work.

But I know you're unhappy with me, Gogo, unhappy for breaking my promises. I'm sorry. But I can apologize until the world is falling apart and it will all be meaningless if you refuse to forgive me.

So we go to mass in the morning. For the first time in so long. I sit on the wooden bench, remembering all the times I sat here beside Gogo and Mama, wondering how to reconcile everything in my life—my love for God, my love for the ancestors, my love of science, my love of traditional ways. Now I have other questions but it is the same problem—how do I reconcile everything in my life?

The priest puts a wafer in my mouth, Jesus melts on my tongue, and I ask him silently for forgiveness and help.

I feel like I've failed everybody. Everybody but God. Him, you can't fail. He is too big for that.

CHAPTER TWENTY

Choosing the Powerless

The afternoon feels like a maze of emotions. I'm just wandering around. The house. The yard. The street in front of my house. I'm avoiding it. The hut. The amadlozi.

Finally, I ask Zi to start cooking phuthu. I take Nhlanhla and head out to my hut. I enter, bowing low to the ancestral spirits. Nhlanhla sits beside me, leaning heavily against me.

I light a fire and sit.

"Mkhulu," I begin. "Gogo." I address all the ancestors who live in my head, one by one. "Please speak to me. About Little Man and Sifiso. About Ahmed and his murder. About this thing of the taxi wars. About the school protests. About South Africa."

They've been shouting in my head for so long—and I suppose it is correct to say that I have been ignoring the cacophony because I couldn't decide if I wanted to hear what they had to say—that it takes awhile for the noise level to subside.

And then I begin to hear them, one by one. They say nothing to me about Little Man or Sifiso or my situation. But they do give me instructions. Actually, it's almost like they have an argument in my head.

You have to stand up for what's right, Gogo says. You must speak out against the violence. It will destroy Imbali.

Babomkhulu isn't so sure. He doesn't address me but rather responds to Gogo. It will be dangerous. The taxi drivers will come for her. The people who killed Ahmed will come for her.

You speak as though I don't know this already, Gogo says. She still must do this thing. Khosi, I raised you to choose what is right.

Our daughter always does what is right, my great-great-grandfather Zulu says. She just must think about it first.

Shhhhh, says my great-great-great grandmother, the one who sent me to the witch to get a goat. You speak as if she isn't human. She can be tempted, like anyone. She can make mistakes.

Cha! Gogo cries. Not my Khosi, you don't know her like I do.

Like you, I've been watching her all my life, she tells Gogo.

OK, OK, amadlozi, you don't need to fight over this, I say.

You mustn't exaggerate, my ancient grandmother says. An argument is not the same as fighting. Your Gogo has a very high opinion of you, as do we all, but we mustn't lie to ourselves. That is the way of true suffering.

But what is the right in this anyway? I ask. People are tired of suffering. They want good jobs. That is why they killed Ahmed. That is why they started the taxi wars. I am not saying they are doing right, I am just saying they have a reason.

This thing is the same everywhere all over the world! Gogo exclaims. People think they deserve what other people have, for all sorts of reasons. Sometimes they are right, they do deserve it, but that doesn't mean they can take take take and think it will all equal out in the end.

The taxi war involves some people trying to maintain control over territory so they have all the profits. Not so different to what white people did to us under apartheid. And they, too, used violence to keep power.

The anger I feel from people towards the Somalis and Chinese is this sense that we, too, should have businesses, money, land. Why should these people from outside of the country come in and profit when we, who have lived here forever, still don't have enough to live?

And then there are the student protests. I am not at university, so I am not involved, but I understand. We all want to be able to achieve our dreams. I can't even matriculate to go on to university because I can't afford the school fees. What would I do if I were faced with the possibility of going to university but no bursary, nothing to help me pay my way? I suppose right now, I'd be grateful even for that chance. I don't have that chance because it's out of my reach. I had to drop out before I even reached that choice.

After all we've suffered, aren't we entitled to a little more?

I don't even voice the question but the amadlozi hear me anyway. And I hear Mkhulu whisper a solid, strong, emphatic No.

And I know he's right. Suffering does not entitle you to anything, just as wealth doesn't protect you from disaster. The sun rises on both evil and good people alike. Rain falls on both the just and the unjust. It is the way of the world. The way of the Lord of the Sky.

Can you guarantee my safety, Mkhulu? I ask.

There is no hillside without a grave, Babomkhulu says.

Death is everywhere then. You cannot avoid it. Thank you, Mkhulu, for your reassuring guarantees.

Don't be sarcastic, mtanami, Gogo says.

What about Zi? I ask. Can you please protect her?

We cannot guarantee her safety either, Gogo says. But you already knew that doing the right thing is sometimes too much dangerous.

It's not a choice between life and doing the right thing, my great-great-grandfather says. If you don't do the right thing, what is life?

I look to my other relative, the querulous one, the one who sent me to the witch. She shrugs her shoulders. Look, she says. Nobody ever said being a sangoma would be easy, did they? Nobody ever said it would be a bed of pillows, did they? Nobody said your life would be all utshwala, mealies, and inyama, did they? The riches pouring in as the people come to you for help? No, no, my girl. A sangoma's life is hard. We do not call the soft or weak to this thing. If you are soft and weak, you must just go now, we do not want you here, you cannot work for us.

I'm not soft and weak, I snap. I think I've proved that by now, nee?

Their voices quelled, I sit, an occasional thump of Nhlanhla's tail the only sound breaking the silence.

We spend so much of our lives avoiding death. But what if that's the wrong way to approach life? What if it's better to live on the razor-edge, right at the margins between life and death, one foot in each world? Then we won't be so afraid to do the right thing, no matter what it costs us.

I think about Madiba, South Africa's most popular, most famous person ever. When he was defending himself during the Rivonia Trials, he said his goal was to fight against domination, all kinds of domination. It was an idea, he claimed, he wanted to live for—but he was prepared to die for it if need be.

He was speaking against apartheid, it is true. But even if apartheid is gone, the truth of what he said is still important today. I will fight against domination of others. That includes taxi drivers against other taxi drivers. And South Africans against the immigrants that live in our lands. Even the government if necessary. It is a question of power, really. Who has power and who is powerless? I will be on the side of the powerless.

I know Zi must be finished now cooking the phuthu and I should go inside but everything is heavy inside me.

Outside, the moon illuminates Imbali. Television lights flicker in homes near and far. A light breeze wafts the scent of grilled meat and vegetables. Through the window, I watch Zi sucking her thumb in front of the TV. She had stopped doing that but after Gogo's death, it started up again, and I haven't yet had the heart to stop her. She's forgotten the phuthu, burning on the stove, the smell assaulting me as soon as I walk inside. I take it off the stovetop and salvage the top layer of maize. I stir-fry some spinach and tomatoes into a gravy to eat with the phuthu and put it in the refrigerator for tomorrow.

"Come watch TV," Zi calls. "Will you fix some peanuts?"

"Wokayi."

So I heat up peanuts on the stovetop, stirring them until they are roasted inside their shells.

We sit on the floor mattress and watch a soapie about a taxi war while we eat. I've always enjoyed the show but I'm not so sure I want to keep watching it now. It reminds me too much of what is going on just outside these doors.

Instead, I keep my eyes on Zi while she eats. She takes tiny, delicate bites, her eyes on the television. Oh, Zi. Precious Zi. I know you said you can't protect her, Gogo, but please. It is hard enough to do this thing without worrying about her at the same time.

CHAPTER TWENTY-ONE

Do not eat the Hair like Lice

After I drop Zi off at school, I walk back to Imbali. The long walk gives me time to think. Or, rather, worry. My head just goes over and over everything.

Makhosi is first on my list of people to visit. Thankfully Thandi and Hopeful are not there so I don't have to pay attention to their needs.

"Welcome, child," she greets me. She is busy tending a large pot, bubbling in the center of the hut over a fire. The air is grey and smoky. "What's on your mind?"

"Makhosi, have you spoken out about the taxi violence?" I ask.

She stops in the middle of stirring the pot and turns around to look at me. "Eh?" she says. "It is no business of mine." Her eyes narrow to small points. "But I understand it is a business of yours. I understand you have other business too, and it is not going well."

"You mean the tuck shop owner who was killed on Friday," I say.

"Yebo. Khosi, I have much to say. You have angered people. How do you expect to make a living as a sangoma if your community turns against you?"

She pauses in her speech to lift a spoonful of murky liquid from the pot. She sniffs it and tastes it. She nods, satisfied, and gestures at me to help her lift the pot of liquid off the fire. We set it to the side and she covers it with a beaded cloth. Then she settles on her mat and wraps herself in a long, colorful cloth.

"The white people have a saying," she says. "I heard it long ago, when

I was working for a madam in Durban, when my children were young. Do not bite the hand that feeds you. And the people, they are the ones who feed you. We have a similar saying in Zulu. Do not eat the hair like lice. The thing that sustains you, you must watch over it and care for it."

I watch her, this gogo who has meant so much to me, this gogo I owe my life and livelihood to. And I realize that I do not completely agree with her. Being a sangoma is about more than pleasing people so that I can eat.

"Thank you, Makhosi," I say. "But I cannot just watch this thing of the taxi war and say nothing. The violence will tear us apart. Could we not—"

"Is that all, young one?" she interrupts.

I have made her angry, by not agreeing with her. And I know it is tradition, for me to always respect her. But respect and truth are not always compatible.

"Yebo, Makhosi," I say. We bow to the ancestral spirits inside each other, and then I make my way out to the street.

I am not entirely sure what I am meant to do next but I make my way to my street. My neighbor MaZondi is toiling up the hill with a sack of groceries. I run to meet her and take the load.

"Ah, thank you, child," she says. MaZondi is the gossip of the street. And she doesn't take long to ask about what is on her mind, what the police have discovered about the dead man. Who killed him and why did they leave him at my doorstep. "It is bad luck," she declares. "The people won't visit a sangoma if dead men keep appearing at your gate like that." She chuckles.

"I know, Mama," I say. "I made somebody angry. But I will not stop telling people the truth. The Somali didn't deserve to die."

"And do we deserve to starve in our own homes?" she asks. "You tell me, should we Zulu be cold so that foreigners can warm themselves with our firewood, stolen right from our own doorstep?"

A part of me wants to shut up, but another part of me plows forward. "Oh, Mama, those questions have nothing to do with this man's death. He did not steal from us."

We've reached her house now. I place her groceries down by the door.

"These men and women from other places, they must just go back and eat their own problems," MaZondi says. "If that means they are hungry, that is not our problem. They should not come and make us hungry so they can eat."

"Oh, Ma—" I start to say.

"Cha!" she cuts me off. "I thank you for carrying my load. You have said your words, now go."

The slamming of her door is like a little exclamation point.

Gogo and Mkhulu, if you meant for me to alienate the world, you have succeeded indeed.

It is my petulant ancestor who responds. The ancestor who arranged for the witch to give me a goat. Eh eh eh, my girl, she exclaims. You are like the angry dog who bites itself when it lashes out. There is no need to feel pity for yourself.

Fine, I tell her. But when they all turn against me, who will be for me?

By this time, I've arrived home. Sifiso, dressed in his police uniform, is leaning against my gate, a box tucked under his arm. "I'm on my lunchbreak," he says. "I hoped to find you home. I'm so glad I waited some few minutes."

A jolt of happiness floods my whole body.

As soon as we are inside, he sets the box down, swings me up in his arms and kisses me. I am not exactly light and his muscles bulge as he lowers me. "Careful, or you will burst the seams in your uniform," I joke.

He leans against the wall, watching me, a little smile on his face. His fingers in mine.

"You look happy," I say. "Content."

His finger traces my jawline, he plays with my earlobe. Leans forward and kisses me again. A shiver down my whole body. It almost eliminates the fear and anger sparked by Makhosi and MaZondi. Almost.

"Come, let's eat." We sit on the floor and he opens the box. Fried chicken from KFC. We open the little containers of potatoes and cole slaw and dig in.

"What are you doing today?" I ask.

"Oh, going here, going there, a little of this, a little of that. I visited Ahmed's widow and children."

"Oh? What are they going to do?"

"One thing you can say about the Somalis," he says, "they take care of each other. She is going to live with her sister in Zambia. They have already organized money for her and the children to get there. They leave tomorrow."

"What does she say about Ahmed's death?"

"She doesn't know anything. But she says the young men were getting bold. They attacked her husband some few weeks ago with knives. They had threatened to come to their house at night and set it on fire with the family inside it. They were already making preparations to leave South Africa when Ahmed was killed."

"Oh, no! That's terrible!" I imagine the fear and anger that must have sparked their decisions—to have come from so far away, seeking a safe place from the ravages of war, only to find more violence.

Sifiso nods. "It is. But I must think of you, too, Khosi. You are part of this. Do you think it is safe for you to stay here?"

"Where would I go?" I ask. "I've always lived here."

Would my neighbors turn against me? I can't believe it but then, somebody must have seen the people who murdered Ahmed and they are saying nothing. I think of Gladys Nene, of her sons—of seeing them near the tuck shop the day the taxi war violence killed two passengers. I shiver, remembering the way they stared at me. Yes, I believe they would do something.

Mkhulu, they are challenging me, I say. They are challenging *you*. I told them I would pray for Ahmed's protection and see what has happened. What they have done to respond to that.

You worry too much, my girl. That voice again. She has a harsh voice but one that you instantly believe.

How can I not worry—a murdered man left at my gate? It was a message.

And they will receive a reply to their message, she says. Trust me, my girl. Do you think we will leave you to fight this alone? You are not alone.

No? I ask.

No, she says firmly. You may not always like us but we will never leave you.

"There is nowhere for you to go?" Sifiso asks. "Truly?"

I turn my attention back to the here-and-now world. To him. To this beautiful man standing in front of me, his fingers trailing down my arm and playing with the end of my shirt where wrist meets hand. "I already told you. Only my auntie and she has accused me of witchcraft."

He sighs. "I don't want you here, in danger, love. I will move back to my mother's house and you and Zi can stay at my house, in town."

My mind moves fast. If we were in town, we would not have to travel far to go to Zi's school. We would see Sifiso, every day perhaps—. No. I like the plan, I like it too much. What about my business? And what about the *amadlozi* telling me that I must speak out about the violence? If I leave, what am I saying about myself? I have wanted to leave for so long and the *amadlozi* have told me no no no. What would they think of this offer? Should I leave? Should I stay?

"Thank you, Sifiso, I really appreciate what you have offered. I'll think about it."

He leans forward and kisses me, a slow kiss that drives all the voices out of my head.

"Don't think about it too long," he urges. "Don't think about it so long that you become another victim, like Ahmed."

When he leaves, it's time to fetch Zi from school. But before I head that direction, I walk up the hill towards Little Man's house. I keep to the side where he's unlikely to see me approach. Anyway, I'm sure he's out working the taxi route. But I don't want his mama to see me either.

I stand in the shadow of his neighbor's house. Little Man's house, like all the houses here, is the same small little matchbox house, RDP, government housing, as my own—except his is yellow instead of pink. It's the sort of house I expect to live in for a long time, though at one time I dreamed of becoming a nurse and living somewhere better.

I watch his front door. I've been in and out of there so many times. His parents are used to me. What has happened? What have we lost? I no longer feel like I can just go up and knock just to say hello, just to see how he's doing, even to find out if he's still alive.

CHAPTER TWENTY-TWO

Delight in His Voice

After a while, you begin to wonder: what is the message they are sending. And I don't mean the amadlozi. It was Makhosi who told me I must have angered the community. Perhaps that is true. Or perhaps they are just scared. But nobody is coming to use my services, and I wonder if I will recover from this thing of Ahmed's murder.

Walking through downtown Pietermaritzburg, on my way home from dropping Zi off, I linger in the crowded streets, thinking. Perhaps I could come here and set up shop. Spread out a blanket and my shells and beads for throwing, wait for people to come. But that is a challenge to other sangomas already practicing here, and I don't think I want to play that game.

So many people are walking, moving this way and that. I pass the taxi rank, and I can't help peering inside to see if Bo's taxi is there, but I see nothing.

Just past the taxi rank, somebody bumps into me. I twirl around as he says, "Sorry, sorry," and then, "Makhosi!"

It takes me a minute to recognize the young man who visited me shortly after Gogo's funeral. At the time, he was wondering why he couldn't find a job or why his wife hadn't fallen pregnant.

He looks radiant, light shining from his eyes.

"Hello, bhuti, how are you?" I ask, though I don't need to ask.

He pumps my hand up and down. "I am well, I am well," he says. "I have meant to come see you for some time now."

"Is it?"

"Yebo impela. I finally found a job and we just found out that my wife is pregnant, two months now. You were right, I spoke to my brother. We cleared things up and we are brothers again. We have even started lobola talks with a woman's family, he will soon be married, and I think that has made a difference. After that, everything fell into place. I must say thank you, thank you."

The words fall out of his mouth with enthusiasm. He can't stop talking. I watch his mouth move and move and finally smile at him to stop the torrent.

"You see, it is not me you must thank," I say. "It is yourself who solved this problem. You were so stressed, it is no wonder you could not find a job or your wife fall pregnant. And you chose to forgive your brother for his jealousy, and that is something only you could do."

"No, no." He puts up a hand to stop me. "No, Makhosi. You discovered the source of the problem, and you pointed the way. Thank you, indeed, thank you."

The encounter leaves me with a warm glow, something I haven't felt much of lately, except when I'm with Sifiso.

Speaking of Sifiso…we haven't spoken since he visited the other day and I miss him. I miss his smile. I miss his voice.

I pull out my phone and dial his number. Of course I have saved him as a contact but I've memorized his number anyway. It feels…important.

"Khosi!" The delight in his voice when he answers the phone makes the bottom of my stomach drop away. I stop, dead still, in the middle of the sidewalk and just let the people walk around me on either side, staring at me as they pass. "Good morning!"

"I'm glad to hear your voice," I say. I start to walk again, crossing the street and heading towards the beautiful red brick city hall. I duck under a jacaranda tree to finish the conversation, realizing suddenly that I don't want anything to distract me from it, even walking or avoiding people.

"Oh, hearing your voice has made my entire day a good one," he says. "And it did not start out well, so that is saying something."

I admit, I have been so preoccupied with my own worries, I have thought little of Sifiso's. That is something to change. "It is still morning," I say. "What has happened?"

"We were called out to a home invasion early this morning," he says. "I will spare you the most gruesome details but it was not a pretty scene. They had hacked off the face of one of the victims. You know, I understand this thing of desperation that drives some men and women to steal, but I do not understand this thing of such terrible anger that leads to—oh, such vicious attacks on others. It seems like such personal anger, even though the victims and attackers were strangers."

"That sounds like a terrible way to start your day," I say. "I'm sorry." I think about this act of anger, to take a person's face. It seems a way to steal your victim's identity, their personhood, their very humanity. That would be a slow-burning simmering anger that erupted in a sudden volcano of violence.

"I would much rather start my day seeing your beautiful face," he says. "Can you send me a picture? I would like to keep one on my phone."

"Oh, my phone doesn't have a camera," I say. "It is just one of these cheap phones. I can text and call, that is all."

He laughs. "Well, I will fix that."

I worry for some few seconds. I do not want Sifiso to think he has to give me things, or buy my love, the way so many men and women think.

"Why are you silent, thando?" Sifiso asks. "It would be my pleasure to get you a better phone, but I do not want you to think you would owe me anything. Do you understand?"

I open my mouth to answer, but I can't the force words out. Tears drip down my cheeks. I don't want Sifiso to know his words have made me cry.

"Khosi? Are you there?" he asks.

I nod, as if he can see me.

"If it makes you uncomfortable," he says, "I will simply snap a photo next time I see you, and we will save the gift of a phone until later, when you are ready. But I would like to give you good things. Is that all-right, someday? Can we work towards that?"

"Yes," I whisper at last. Whispering is the only thing I trust my voice to do.

After we hang up, I stay in my place under the tree for some few minutes. Across the way is the statue of Gandhi, reminding us all of the legacy of justice in this city. I wonder what Gandhi would make of Pietermaritzburg now, more than a hundred years after he visited, after he spent a night in the train station realizing he needed to stand up for himself? I wonder what he would make of Pietermaritzburg today, of all the crime, of all the poverty, of a home invasion that ends with somebody's face hacked off? I have heard it said "no justice, no peace." We haven't yet seen justice in our land, and so we haven't yet seen peace.

The phone call with Sifiso has left me shaken in more ways than one.

I realize he is making me think even more about this world we live in. And he is making me think about what I expect and want in a relationship. This thing with Sifiso, it is more than just chills and my stomach dropping and liking the way he makes me feel. I am really beginning to care about him, care for him. I don't know where that leaves me. I don't know what I should think, or what I should do now. I suppose I will just keep putting one foot in front of the other and letting them lead, letting them go where they will.

CHAPTER TWENTY-THREE

NOT SO SECRET SECRET

MaDudu calls to us from her side of the fence when we get home from school some few days later. Zi goes inside and lets Nhlanhla out while I head over to have a short chat. We talk through the metal openings, Nhlanhla settling in to the dust, lying at my feet. She presses against my legs, a small warm brown comfort.

"I chased away two men who were rattling and rattling your gate while you were gone," she greeted me. "Sho! Nhlanhla was barking like a mad dog inside."

"Who were they? What did they want?"

She shook her head. "I've never seen them before. I asked what they needed and why they were here and when they told me to mind my own business, I told them to go away or I would call the police."

I glance at my gate, glad Sifiso brought me a new lock. "What do you think I should do?"

"You should call your uncle and tell him to come home," she advises. "You shouldn't be alone."

"Oh no, Ma, you know my uncle thinks I used witchcraft against Gogo."

"Does he?" she says. "Shame." And for a moment, she looks like she feels shame for herself all over again, remembering the time from before Mama died when she employed the witch against us. Wow, how things have changed. "Or can you move in with your baba?" she asks.

I shake my head.

"Where is Little Man? Couldn't he come stay here for some few days?"

It's unexpected but as soon as she asks that one thing, tears start rolling down my cheeks, and once they start, they don't stop.

MaDudu reaches a bony hand through the gap in our fences and grabs my hand. "Mtanami, I did not mean to cause you sorrow," she says.

"Cha, I know," I wail. "Little Man is mad at me and you know, he works for a khumbi…"

"No!" She sounds shocked. "Is he caught up in this thing, the taxi war?"

I can't speak. I just nod, tears soaking my cheeks.

"But he will end up dead or in prison," she exclaims.

I bow my head, wiping the tears away, trying to get ahold of myself. I've never been this emotional, I've always been able to control it, what is happening to me?

"That is what I'm afraid of," I whisper at last.

"He must stop," she says. "You must tell him. He must stop being so selfish, he must think about you, about you and this thing." She puts her hand to her mouth, realizing she said too much.

"What what what?" I ask. "You know about this thing?"

"Mtanami, I had six of my own, do you think I do not recognize the signs?" She laughs, a bit of the cackle in her laughter, then gestures towards my stomach. "I don't need to be a sangoma to divine this thing of falling pregnant."

"Oh, no," I say. "I haven't told anyone. But if *you* know…"

"No, no," she says. "It is early yet and I am around you more than most people. Do not worry about the others. But tell me, do you know when you fell pregnant?"

"Just after Gogo passed…" I say. "It is maybe fifteen or sixteen weeks now." Fresh tears start to fall. "What am I going to do?"

The look on her face is kind but perplexed at the same time. "You'll do what all we Zulu women do," she says. "You'll bear this burden and you'll love your child more than life itself."

"Of course," I say. "I meant, what should I do right now? Who should I tell? What am I going to do?"

"The first person you need to tell is Little Man," she advises. "Perhaps it is just what he needs to stop this thing of foolishness. Taxi wars! What is he thinking? And then the two of you can make a plan. I will help with whatever you decide."

I look at my feet, ashamed to find myself in this predicament. "What do you think Mama and Gogo would do, if they were still here?"

MaDudu touches my arm. "They would prepare the house for a baby," she says. "What else do you think they would do?"

Her touch makes me want to put my head on her shoulder. But I don't. I can't.

"Before she died, Gogo made me promise I wouldn't do this very thing I've done. Be with Little Man, get serious, fall pregnant. She wanted me to finish school and wait a few years to get married and have children. And here I am, not even in school, not married, and now this baby—and she's only been gone four months. Do you think she's very angry with me?"

"Khosi." MaDudu bows her face and I see just how old she has become. Why must the people we love grow old quick quick? "Do I need to remind you that you are a sangoma? If you think she's angry with you, or if you want to know what she thinks you should do, why don't you go into your hut and ask? She will tell you."

That seems simple enough but it isn't something I feel capable of doing just yet. I talk to you all the time, Gogo, but you and I, we avoid this topic. How I broke both the promises I made to you. Perhaps that I am a disappointment. Shame, I'm afraid of what you'll say. I cannot.

Instead, Zi and I eat—toasted bread with Rama and jam that I find in the back of the cupboard—and then take a nap. I'm exhausted.

CHAPTER TWENTY-FOUR

MY GIRL

I wake to the sound of thunder and rain thudding on the roof. My head aches, my mouth tastes strange. The thought of eating bread with Rama and jam ever again makes me sick to my stomach. Zi's still asleep so I go into the kitchen and drink two full glasses of water, terribly thirsty.

I've missed a call from Sifiso. I know I should try to call Little Man. It's been—so long. I've thought about calling every day since our fight. I think about it for some few minutes and then I call Sifiso. I'm not going to question my motives right now. I just do it.

"Heyyyy," he answers on the first ring. "How's my girl?"

Am I his girl? It's true, it already feels like I am.

"Are you working?"

"No, I have the afternoon off," he says. "I'm visiting my mother. Can I come by and see you? I have a shift starting at six."

I glance at the clock. It's four. "I'd like that," I say, feeling shy.

"I'll be there now now."

Now that it's set he's coming, I'm full of nervous energy. I brush my teeth to get rid of the metallic taste—a taste that I'm beginning to realize might be "pregnant mouth"—and start to clean the already-clean kitchen.

And now I should call Little Man. I sigh, dreading that call but needing to make it too—needing to connect or disconnect, one or the other. What if he answers the phone? What if he never answers? I text instead. *How are you, Little Man?*

It seems all awkward and formal, but I don't know what else to write. Everything is all wrong and not because of Sifiso. Because of Little Man getting mad at me and storming away and not ever coming back. Because of my being pregnant. Because of the taxi wars.

So I add, quickly, *Are you still mad at me?* A little more natural. But also a stupid question. Of course he's still mad at me. That's why he hasn't shown up for four weeks. And then, because of MaDudu, I text, *We need to talk. Can you come by tomorrow?*

My stomach hurts just thinking about talking to him. I mean, what do I say to him?—I fell pregnant, I met someone else, please quit your job because I'm afraid you're going to end up in jail or dead and I'm not sure which is worse, are we finished? I need to say goodbye, Little Man. I need an end to 'us.' I still love you, Little Man. Or maybe, Hey, no matter what happens with us, this baby is going to show up in some few months. We have to talk about what that means.

He still hasn't answered when the gate rattles, Nhlanhla bursts into happy little barks, and I look outside to see Sifiso. Water mists down from the sky. His face breaks into the most goofy grin when I open the door and head out to greet him.

As soon as I open the gate, his arms circle my waist and his lips are whispering in my ear, "I'm so glad to see you, I missed you."

My heart is beating hard and my breath is uneven and I hug him back. He's strong, lean, muscles in all the right places. It feels good to put my arms all the way around him, to feel his arms around me. I put my hand on his head, his hair wet from the lightly falling rain.

He squeezes me gently. I squeeze back.

"Come inside," I say, afraid he might kiss me right out here in front of God and everybody.

He catches my hand and holds it as we cross the yard. I look at MaDudu's house and see the curtain in her kitchen window move the tiniest bit.

The secret's out. I'm going to have to deal with this now.

And it's true, as soon as we step inside the house, he swings me around and holds me again, kissing my hair. His lips nibble my ear and then my neck and my whole body relaxes into him.

I stay very still, not wanting to move, not wanting this moment to end. Wanting to be here, forever.

Until I hear a small voice. "Khosi?"

I whirl out of his arms.

Zi stands in the hallway. She's scowling at us.

"Sifiso just stopped by to say hi," I say, hoping to prevent the deluge kodwa…it's too late for that.

"I miss Little Man," she announces. "Where is Little Man?"

My heart drops a million kilometers.

"Who's Little Man?" Sifiso says.

Nobody answers. Zi looks at me accusingly.

"Is he a friend? An old boyfriend?" He has a million questions in his eyes but he doesn't seem angry. Not yet.

I was his girl for all of a few days, or hours, maybe. Tears prick my eyelids. "We should talk about it. But not in front of Zi."

"I see," he says. He's still smiling but suddenly it seems a little forced.

"I'm hungry," Zi says. "Starving. What's for dinner, Khosi?"

"Let's go to Spur," Sifiso whispers. "The restaurant with the gigantic Indian chief logo? Have you eaten there?"

I nod. I've never eaten there but I know the restaurant he's talking about. There is one right around the corner in Edendale Mall.

"They have a play area for kids. Zi can play there and you and I can talk while she's busy. I'll drop you off back home before going to work."

"Are you sure?" I ask.

He nods so we head out the gate, leaving Nhlanhla outside.

We order chicken and chips and cool drinks. Zi runs off to play in the children's area. Left alone with Sifiso, I don't know where to look. I contort the napkin into a horrendous shape until he reaches across the table and places his hand over mine. When I look up, his mouth is twisted—partly a smile, partly a frown, and it hurts just looking at it.

"You are too young to be married," he says, "so unless that is what you are about to tell me…"

"No," I say, a relieved laugh escaping my lips. "I'm not married."

"Thank God," he says, rolling his eyes towards the ceiling.

"Are *you* married?"

"I thought I already told you that," he says. "No, I have never been married. I am free. Well, I was a week ago… Now my heart belongs to you."

I smile at the table. At the same time, hurting inside, the secrets inside forming a strong, hard knot.

He reaches across the table, lifts my chin until I'm looking at him. He leans over and kisses me. Gently.

I look at him. Sifiso.

"Who is Little Man?" he asks.

"He was my best friend," I say, honestly. "And my boyfriend until some few weeks ago. We had a fight and he walked out on us. I haven't heard from him since and I—. So I don't know anymore. I think it's over. He's—he works for a taxi driver—"

He withdraws his hands from mine and holds one up to stop me. "Oh," he says, his voice flat. He looks away, towards the play room where Zi is playing. "That is not good," he says.

"I know," I say in a small voice. But I don't know if he means it's not good that I have a maybe-boyfriend or that he works for a taxi.

We sit in silence for a few minutes. There's a funny thing about silence. The longer you sit in it, the louder it grows. A cacophony of voices is cackling in my head, all the ancestors yelling at me, so loud I practically can't hear them. They're shouting something…something…a word I can't quite catch…

"I fell pregnant," I whisper.

He reaches across the table and grips my hand, his grip firm but still gentle. The look on his face is intent, sincere. "Do you think *that* matters to me?"

I look into his eyes—a lighter brown than expected, with almost a green tint to them—and I relax into their kindness.

"I love babies," he says.

"I didn't know," I admit.

"I would, especially, love *your* baby," he says.

We are silent.

"What are we going to do?" he asks finally.

"What do you want to do?" I ask.

He smiles and though his smile is still as open as before, it's also a little broken. "You already know what I want," he says. "That hasn't changed just because—just because the timing is inconvenient. Just because of—this." He gestures towards my stomach. "The only question that matters is what do *you* want?"

I think about all the things Little Man has always done for me and how he has always been there for me. Until recently, in any case. And how he is the father of the baby I'm carrying. And I look at this beautiful man across from me. The one who says that doesn't matter to him. "I know what I want to do but I don't know if it's the right thing," I say.

He sighs. "I'm wondering if I should ask what you want to do, whether what you want to do would be in my favor or Little Man's." He shakes his head. "I'm not going to ask. And I'm not going to tell you what to do," he adds, quick quick. "But I do want you to think very carefully. You know the taxi wars—they're getting more and more violent each day?"

I nod.

"Even if your Little Man still has his hands clean at the moment… unless he gets out of it now—and by that I mean, he needs to get out *now now*—he's not going to have clean hands much longer. You have to think about this carefully. You have to think about your future. Is that what you would want—for him? For your child?"

I whisper, "I think it might be too late already." I add, "It is only a suspicion but I don't think he has clean hands anymore."

He leans forward, his voice suddenly urgent, and he clutches my hands and grips them, warm, passionate. "Then get out," he says. "Get out while you can, before he becomes too dangerous to be around, before you get associated with his business and the things he does. Get out and…choose me. Choose me, Khosi. I promise I'll never—" He breaks off and grips the side of the table. "I'm a good man, Khosi," he finishes. "I'm a good man."

Tears flow freely down my face and drip off my nose. One splashes onto his hand.

"Eish," he says. "Listen to me. I'll take you home. And I'll leave you alone, for now, and let you think. But I'll come back to find out the answer. I hope it's yes. We could be good together. I will always be the man you see in front of you right now."

The server brings our food. Sifiso fetches Zi from the playroom and the three of us eat, though the food is tasteless to me. Now that we've had our talk, Sifiso is almost cheerful and certainly talkative. He and Zi carry the conversation, but I don't follow it. I'm too busy thinking.

CHAPTER TWENTY-FIVE

SEPARATED FROM THE HERD

Sifiso drops us off with a reminder that he'll be back with another officer in a day or two to continue investigating Ahmed's murder. He gives me a quick squeeze with a hurried whisper, "Don't make me wait too long for your answer."

Nhlanhla greets us at the gate as though nothing is wrong. But the lock Sifiso gave me has been cut off with some sort of bolt cutter and is lying in the dirt.

Immediately, Zi and I look to see if tsotsis have been here and robbed us.

The front door is closed and locked.

We walk slowly around the house looking for signs of muthi. The dirt in the front yard is scuffed and there are tire tracks, but I see nothing that would make me think an umthakathi left a curse on us.

Zi and I walk in the door, and that is when we know that we have been robbed after all. Because the TV is gone. So is the mattress that was on the floor, that we were using for a sofa.

"Hheyi, what is this?" I ask. I look at Nhlanhla. "What is going on? You are a useless dog."

Nhlanhla whines.

"Oh, don't think I'm going to apologize to you," I tell her. "You are supposed to protect the house. That is your job."

Zi starts running through the house. "Gogo's clothes are all gone," she announces. I follow her into our room and see that the drawer with Gogo's clothes is open and completely empty. My own drawer is full of clothes and so is Zi's. So they wanted Gogo's things only.

We go into the kitchen. Gogo's pink plastic chair, the cracked one—it is gone. I open the cupboards. The big bag of mealies is still there but cups and dishes—they are gone. I open the fridge. The box of milk is still there, and somebody kindly dumped out the contents of the big pot of phuthu, so at least the food is still here—but the big pot we use to cook it in is gone.

I suppose I can be grateful that they left the food.

I think I know what has happened but I need to verify it before I accuse anybody.

"Wait here," I tell Zi, and I go outside and rattle the gate until MaDudu comes outside.

She's tying a head cloth around her head, hurrying, and she greets me as though she needs to just hurry through the greeting. "Hawu, Khosi," she half-shouts, half-pants. "You must be wondering..."

"Yebo," I say, "who was here? What happened? Must I call the police?"

"Oh, little one, it was your auntie and her husband," she says. "They came with a bolt cutter. They took away some few things in his bakkie."

Of course, they have met Nhlanhla, and they have a key to the place, so that is why she behaved as though nothing were wrong.

"I came out and asked them what they were doing," MaDudu continues. "They said that though they could not have the house, they were simply taking the rest of Gogo's things, which rightfully belong to them. What could I do, my child? It is tradition."

My shoulders droop. "Couldn't they wait until I was here?"

"I asked them the same question, mtanami," she says. And then she lowers her voice, as though people might be listening, though there is nobody around. "Your auntie said she would rather die than see you again. She told me I should also be worried, living next door to a witch. I told her you were not a witch, and she laughed and said you have bewitched me also." MaDudu is telling me all of these things and she knows me but way back, I sense that she is frightened.

"You don't believe her, do you, Gogo?" I ask.

"Oh, no," she says, and the fear is replaced with a flame of indignant pride. "No, no, no! You, Khosi Zulu, an umthakathi? Never! But I fear for you. They are very angry with you, your family, they are very angry over these things. And anger is like a hungry snake, it just eats the rat whole. My child, it makes me wonder what they are willing to do to bring you to your knees."

This is the thing I wonder also.

I go inside and explain to Zi that Auntie Phumzile came back for the rest of Gogo's things. And then I sit on the floor of the living room, back against the wall, staring at the empty space where the TV used to sit.

I suppose I have been hoping that someday soon, a big wind of common sense would blow across my auntie's anger, and she would come to me and say, Let us let this thing lie. We are family. We must be family again.

But now I know, that was foolishness. Zi and I, we are like the common cattle, separated from the herd, alone in the world without a family.

Ngikhathele, I'm so tired, I want to curl up into a big ball and sleep until next week.

CHAPTER TWENTY-SIX

The Reckoning

But of course I don't sleep. No, no, I stay awake all night, realizing a simple truth. It is time to face all the problems in my life. And the main problem is Little Man. If he won't answer my texts, and he isn't coming by to see me, I'll go to him.

The next day, instead of taking Zi to school, we wait until mid-morning and then, despite the rain and the mud, we walk up the hill towards Little Man's house. It's not far, about a fifteen-minute walk, but I go slow. Partly so we don't slip, partly just to give myself enough time for what I'm facing. Walking up to Little Man's house always makes me think about how far we've come and now, apparently, how far we still have to go. Because whatever is going to happen next, Little Man will always be a part of my life. It's time I told him why.

Zi holds my hand and walks quietly beside me. This is completely uncharacteristic of her and I find myself glancing at her from time to time, wondering what's going on inside her head. Zi is one of these exuberant little girls, so loud you never stop to think that she has her own thoughts kept up inside her.

I've never asked her to tell me what she thinks. For example, what did she think about when Mama died? Or, more recently, Gogo's death? We cried together, but I did not ask her to tell me how she felt. Why not? It is my business to find out what people think and feel, that is a big part of what healing is all about, but *I'm* afraid of my nine-year-old sister's feelings!

The road is slick with water and our shoes are soon tacky from the mud. They make a thick sound like the X in Zulu, the sound of the tongue clicking against the inside of the cheek. The only other sound is the soft hiss of rain as it plops on the ground.

We pass the place where Little Man kissed me for the first time. It's nothing special—a fence on the side of the road, an open field behind it, but it hid us from prying eyes. That was three years ago. I was only fourteen and he was fifteen. By the time he kissed me, we'd known each other a long time and I already knew he'd be in my life...well—forever.

No matter what happens with Sifiso, that is the truth. Little Man is the father of the child I am carrying. He must be part of this, part of me, always.

"Khosi," Zi breaks the silence.

"Ja?"

"I like Sifiso," she says.

"Yes," I agree.

"I like his laugh," she says.

"Oh?" I say. "Why?"

"It has kindness in it."

Her words are hard little stones pelting my tender skin.

We continue in silence again. Then: "I'm sorry," she says.

"Why are you sorry?" I want to be angry with her but I don't have it in me. Right now, I just have to think about what to say to Little Man.

"I'm sorry if I ruined it," she says. "By asking about Little Man."

"Eh," I grunt. I don't know what else to say.

She sighs loudly, in between the ticky-tacky sound of her shoes lifting from the mud's clutch.

"Kulungile," I finally say, just so she feels better. "I do not believe you can say 'what happens is meant to be,' because if that is true, it means we are not responsible for the bad choices we make. But I do know the ancestors have something to say about all of this."

That reminds me that I have a lot to talk to them about: Sifiso and Little Man. Ahmed. My schooling. The baby, the one I've been ignoring in all my conversations with them.

But first, I have to do this thing. So again, I put one foot in front of the other and keep walking.

Little Man's mother comes to the door, hand to her mouth. Whenever I see her, I catch my breath a little. If she was a man, she'd look exactly like Little Man. He carries her face on his shoulders, but in every other way, he is like his Baba, a man I only met once.

"Sawubona, ninjani, Khosi," she greets me. Then she looks behind her, over her shoulder, like she's worried about somebody in the house overhearing us.

"Is Little Man here?" I ask.

She shakes her head no and looks left and right, checking the surroundings. Then she lowers her voice: "He's in hospital."

"What?" My voice sounds unnecessarily loud. She waves her hands around as if to remind me to quiet down.

"Somebody shot him," she whispers.

"Who? When?"

"I don't know. It is two days now."

Two days already? And I am just now learning about it?

"Why didn't you call me?" I demand. I'm on the edge of tears. She can see it. I can't let her see me cry though. If Little Man and I ever have a future together, I will be her makoti—the daughter-in-law—and she must never see I am weak because she will use it against me. I will already lack power in her family.

She looks at the ground, though, and that tells me all I need to know about the state of things between me and Little Man.

"I would have come," I say, but my anger is like shaking a spear in the wind. It will do no good. "I would have prayed for him," I say, more quietly this time. "Tell me what you know. Was he working at the time? For Bo?"

She nods and again looks around. Fearful. They must be watching.

"Tell me," I say.

She shakes her head. Helpless. "If you want to visit him, go. He's at Edendale. I don't know if he'll be glad to see you or not…"

Her voice trails off and the door closes behind her. I rock back and forth on my heels. What now? What now? Tears drip down my face. All this time, I've been mad at him and he's been in hospital...he could have died and I wouldn't have known...

But her last words sink in. Little Man might not be glad to see me, all because of our stupid fight. All because I didn't think my sister would be safe riding in a taxi that, I am sorry to say now, clearly was not safe.

I'm not sure who should be the target of the sudden anger flooding my entire being. Little Man, for not calling me from the hospital? His family, for not telling me? The ancestors, for keeping all of this secret? Little Man for the way he's been behaving? And I thought we were so connected. Connected forever. Even this little baby buried deep inside me can't do that if nobody else reaches out a hand to keep the connection alive.

Zi puts her hand in mine. "Woza, Khosi, let's go."

I follow her, numb, not thinking about where we're going until I look up and realize we have passed the road to our house and are walking towards the main road that goes up to the hospital.

"Where are we going?" I ask.

"We have to visit him," Zi says.

I glare at her. "We don't *have to* do anything, Zi!"

She plants her little feet firmly on the ground and glares right back at me. I suck in my breath. Just like Little Man looks like his mother, Zi looks like Mama. The same beautiful, vivacious face. The same stubbornness. "You have to do this," she insists.

I don't know if she's right or not but I don't have the will to resist. So we keep going. Down the hill, then following the road up the hill to Edendale. Tiny rivulets of rain water rush past in the ditch beside us. I watch the flowing trickle as we trudge up the hill.

The hospital's red-brick building looks dreary to me in the hazy smog of mid-day and misty rain. We enter to even bleaker décor, a long hallway with a checkered floor and mint green walls. Although it's clearly clean, something about the way it smells makes me want to turn around and leave. So much for wanting to be a nurse…a dream that dies a little more every single day I'm not in school anyway…

The security guard at the front desk directs us to Little Man's room and tells us that visiting hours end in fifteen minutes. So we hurry through the desolate halls, searching for his room. The fact that we can visit him fills me with hope, even as I dread seeing him. *What am I going to say? What is he going to say?*

He's sleeping, a shock of his curly hair sticking straight up like a pillar.

When I first met Little Man, it was his dreadlocks I fell for, his easy smile, the respectful and funny way he talked to me. Asleep, I see none of that, just the gentle way his face is aging into the man he's becoming—an uneasy marriage between the funny, kind boy I have always known and something harder and willing to fight.

His right arm is heavily bandaged and an IV feeds him fluids.

Zi stands at the foot of his bed while I take the chair beside him, wondering if I should wake him up or leave him alone. He shifts in his sleep and I can't help it, I reach out for his hand.

His eyes fly open.

"Little Man," I whisper.

He jerks his hand away and closes his eyes again. "Go away," he says.

"What?" I hear what he says but I can't believe he said it.

"Go away," he says. "You don't care about me anyway."

I'm silent for a full minute, biting back the stream of angry words. The room smells astringent mixed with that terrible yellowish smell of the ill and the dying, something that can never be scrubbed clean no matter how much disinfectant you use.

"If I didn't care," I say, making my voice as steady as possible, "I wouldn't bother fighting with you. You don't fight with people unless, in some way, you care."

A tear trickles down the side of his face.

"And I wouldn't be here if I didn't care," I add.

Zi opens her mouth. I reach out and put my hand over her lips. I don't know what she's about to say but God help her if she tells him I almost didn't come to visit. She brushes my hand away.

"We miss you, Little Man," she says. "Where have you been?"

Eyes still closed, his fingers grope across the sheet until he finds my hand. He grips it, hard, like he's never going to let go. "Thanks for coming," he says. After a brief pause, "Thanks for not leaving when I told you to go." He is silent for a long while and then says, "I miss you."

I should tell him I miss him too, which is true, but I am afraid to say it because of what it might mean or what it might do. Should I try to fix this rift between us? I swallow back the words forming in response. "What happened?" I ask instead.

His words tumble out, thick and dull, as though his tongue is swollen—but maybe it's just his attempt to keep back the flood of tears. "Happy, one of Langa's men, shot me while we were fleeing."

I don't ask why they were fleeing. Why, because I'm a coward.

I want to reach out and touch his hand but hold myself back. "Where did the bullet hit you?"

"The bullet went straight through my arm," he says. "Shredded the bone. They say it's minced, like meat. The docs want to cut it open, mess around, see what they can fix. I'm supposed to enter the surgery theatre in the morning…"

"Does it hurt?" Zi asks.

He smiles at her and there's something so weary in that smile—so old like he's eighty instead of eighteen—that I feel tears prick the corners of my eyes. "Yebo, but they have been giving me pain killers so it's not so bad."

"Eish, Little Man. This is terrible," I say. "What are you going to do?"

"What else can I do?" Suddenly, he struggles as though he wants to sit up. "Hey! Will you take a message to Bo?"

"That depends," I say slowly. "What's the message?"

Little Man's voice drops to a half-whisper. "Langa's here too, three doors down. I saw them wheel him in."

My heart stands still. "Why does Bo need to know that?"

Little Man shrugs. "I just think he'll be curious, that's all." The lie rolls off his tongue so easily…

"Do you think I'm stupid?" I ask, my angry words like teeth, biting.

"Khosi, no! You've always been the smartest girl I know." His shocked act hardens the anger in my heart.

"Then tell me why would Bo need to know that Langa is in the hospital, three doors down from you? Is it so that Bo can take over Langa's turf while he's sick? Or will he send somebody to the hospital to finish Langa off?"

"Maybe Bo would like to pray for Langa's soul." He grins, a shaky grin that masks deception.

"Do you think this is a joke?" I ask. "Do you think this is *funny*?"

The amadlozi whisper whisper whisper but one word from Mkhulu is abundantly clear: Hamba.

I grab Zi's hand and yank her towards the door. "Come," I say. "We're leaving."

"Khosi, don't be like that," he pleads.

"Be like what?" I shout.

Hamba hamba hamba.

"Do you want me to sit by and say nothing while you take both of our lives and throw them away?" I keep yelling. "And for what? For a job you'll only keep for a few months longer before you're dead or in prison? Ngeke! Ngiyabonga but no thank you."

I stalk out of the room, dragging Zi behind me. I don't say sala kahle or anything. Because I don't want him to sala kahle. He doesn't need to stay well, he needs to stay badly hurt because it might force him to change.

"Khosi?" Zi says outside the door.

"Yebo?"

"What...what were you doing? Was that—goodbye?"

I take a big gulp of air into my lungs, all that deadly hospital air, and release it. Somewhere inside, a deep, nameless ache suggests that goodbye is the truth.

"I think so," I admit.

"Will I ever see him again?" she asks in a lost little voice, the same lostness that I feel.

I don't have an answer for her. "Woza." I tug her hand and she follows, a tear rolling down her cheek.

I'm so relieved to be out of that stifling room. It hurts that I'm so glad to be away from Little Man, I've never felt that way before.

A queer loneliness pricks my heart.

The hallway corridor is empty. We progress slowly, glancing inside. It takes me a few doors before I realize I'm looking for Langa.

A few doors down, there he is. He's hooked up to even more machines than Little Man, and his head is bandaged. Did they shoot him in the head? And by "they," was it Bo or Little Man who shot him?

What will I do if I find out that Little Man was the shooter? Is that something I could possibly forgive? Even condone? The truth forces itself up between my lips in a sudden explosive *Cha. No!* If he has done this thing, he must pay.

Zi puts her hand in mine and we watch the tall, thin man, his chest moving up and down in rhythm to his even breathing. He still hasn't stirred. The big man, the dangerous man, the one that people in the township are afraid of, looks vulnerable and alone, hooked up to machines, blood seeping through his head bandage.

I step inside, circle the bed, watching him carefully. And then I start to pray, the words I memorized long ago as a child in church falling from my lips. At long last, the protective charm he requested and which I did not feel I could give... But seeing him now...the words form on my lips.

"Lord of the Skies, protect him. Protect him from the terror of the night, Lord, and the arrow that flies by day. Protect him from the pestilence that stalks in darkness. Protect him from the destruction that lays waste at noon."

Using some of the lavender water I keep in the pouch by my side, I make the sign of the cross over the doorpost.

Langa senses the movement and his head shifts ever so slightly, just long enough for me to see fear flood his face. He opens his mouth and starts screaming at the top of his lungs.

"What are you doing here, you witch?" he screams.

"No, no—" I start to say.

"Get out!" he screams. "Get out get out get out!"

Zi grabs my wrist and we whirl through the halls, down the stairs, out into the open air. And there, just outside the front entrance, is MaNene, wheeling in a young man in a wheelchair.

"Mama!" I'm shocked into speaking. I look closely at the man she's wheeling in. Her son. Or one of them, at least.

She shrinks back. Moves in front of the wheelchair, shielding her son with her body. "Wena!" she screams. As though I'm going to hurt him. "Leave him alone!" she cries.

"I'm not going to do anything to him," I say. I feel bewildered. Between Langa and now her… "What happened to him?"

"What do you mean, what happened to him?" she yells. "You of all people, you ask this?"

She jerks him forward now, as though to show off his limp body, his useless limb encased in bandages.

"This is your work, you witch! He was shot during a taxi run. You think I don't know you did it? Wena, you said you'd come after us if my sons did anything they shouldn't. I never should have come to you." Her sobs shake her whole body.

"Mama…" That's the only thing I can say.

She starts running inside so fast, her son jerks around in the wheelchair, a flopping doll. He looks like he might fall out.

I gasp and lean over. I retch and retch. Dry heaves, gasps that rack me from head to toe. A long sliver of silver drool dangling from my lips. My whole body, wanting to empty itself. But nothing comes.

CHAPTER TWENTY-SEVEN

Hamba

They wake me in the middle of the night with just one word, the same word they spoke to me when I started this journey three years ago. Hamba.

Where we'll go, I don't know, but I know better than to hesitate. I place jugs of water and packages of Marie biscuits in a thick bag that belonged to Gogo, something Auntie overlooked or did not want.

I wake Zi gently.

"What's going on, Khosi?" she asks, rubbing her eyes.

"We're leaving for a few hours…or days…or weeks," I say. "We have things we must do."

"What?" She's wide awake now, struggling to get out of bed. Her little fingers, surprisingly strong, grip my arm, as if I'm going to disappear—or leave without her. I gather her in my arms and then put on her school backpack—filled instead with supplies—over her winter jacket.

I lock the house carefully, making sure all the lights are out. With Nhlanhla at our side, we step out of the gate in the darkness of the night.

I take very little because I know that the ancestors will take care of us, since they are the ones that called. Yet I cannot help but look behind me at the house. Will we ever return?

The streets are completely empty, not even tsotsis are out at this hour. Taking Zi's hand, we head out into the unknown.

Sometimes you are surprised at what the amadlozi tell you to do, where they lead you. When you set off, you don't know where you're going but somehow you end up exactly where you were meant to be.

And here I am again, at the witch's house, at the top of the hill.

The witch's yard is littered with concrete statues—a graceless lightning bird, lurching into flight; a mischievous dwarf, the tokoloshe; and a series that depicts a girl who, as she dances, slowly turns into a snake. A lion's tail and a full set of shark's teeth, mouth included, dangle on a string over her stoop, just out of reach of the large Rhodesian Ridgeback trotting back and forth in front of the gate.

This is the kind of medicine I could never practice. I ask you, what possible good could come from killing animals to harness their power? Would you be seeking peace? Accountability? Responsibility? Or reconciliation? No, the only thing you can seek with these parts of animals is more violence.

Was it you? I ask my ancestor who first sent me here, so long ago, to get the goat for Gogo's cleansing. The one I recognize as a great-great-great-grandmother, way back. Are you the one who sent me here?

Ehhe, she agrees. Yes, my girl, it was me.

Who is this woman, this umthakathi? I ask. Who is she to me?

Of course I remember, all those years ago, when she dragged me into the spiritual world and tried to turn me into her zombie. But why did she target me then? And why is this ancestor of mine determined to send me to her?

She is my sister's child's child, she answers.

And I realize it in disbelief. We have a common ancestor. My grouchy ancestor, she can speak to us both. The witch and I are connected, forever and ever.

I stare at the world in front of me. No wonder there was a goat waiting for me when I needed it.

The witch's dog growls and bares his teeth at us. Nhlanhla, never one to back down even if she's smaller than the dog in question, parks herself in front of the gate and grins at the fierce dog, as if she knows that's driving him nuts.

"Thula!" the old woman yells at the dog to shut up. She limps out of her hut, practically unchanged from three years ago, wearing a print cloth wrapped around her body. I remember the way a gold tooth flashed in her mouth. If I didn't know better, I'd look at her and just think *old woman* and I would call her Gogo out of respect. If she was wearing her headdress, I would recognize her as a sangoma and call her Makhosi.

She stops and gazes at me and Zi, standing just outside her gate, then shuffles to the gate, shaking her head, tutting. "What is *she* doing here?" she murmurs to herself or probably to her own gogo or Babomkhulu. We may understand the nature of our work differently—the end purposes—but we both have voices in our head that refuse to thula.

"What are *you* doing here?" she demands, grabbing the fence with both hands and shaking it until it rattles. This sends her dog into a new paroxysm of barking. She swats it with the back of her hand. He lays down at her feet and whines.

"Oooh." Zi winces. She doesn't say it but we both feel for that poor dog.

"Eh? What are you doing here?" she shouts at me.

"Angaz," I say. "The ancestors said go, so I went. They said come this way, so I came. I'm as surprised as you that I ended up here."

"I'm not surprised," she says. "Nothing surprises me anymore."

She peers at me, squinting as though the sun were out, and I suddenly realize that she's gone blind in one eye. Her grin reveals blackened gums where several of her teeth have fallen out. The gold tooth that used to distinguish her with its tell-tale glint? Completely gone.

"What is it that you want?" she asks, suddenly suspicious. "I don't do the kinds of things I used to do, not anymore."

The lion tail and shark's teeth dangling from the roof of her hut suggest she's lying. But maybe they are just leftovers from her old life.

"I don't want anything like that," I say.

She looks down her nose at Zi. "But I could use a girl like her to help me around here," she shouts suddenly. "What do you want to trade her for?"

Zi grabs my hand with a rock-hard grip.

"I'm not here to trade my sister," I say.

She snorts. "A sister is of no use to you," she says. "But a zombie who will do your bidding, who will do all your work? If you don't want to leave her here with me, you can pay me and I'll turn her into a zombie for you."

She's fixed Zi with her good eye and Zi seems frozen into place.

I step between them, shielding my little sister. "I have no use for a zombie."

"Ehhe and you have no use for wealth either," she snaps. "And you're able to get all your own work done too without asking for help." She grabs a tuft of my hair, yanking it so hard, my ear is level with her mouth. "If you came to spy on me and steal my secrets, I've already put a curse on you."

She releases my hair so suddenly, my head yanks backward. She looks at me, a strand of my hair caught in between her fingers, and grins. With one of my hairs, she can cast any kind of spell she wants to gain power over me.

I'm in her grip already, I feel it, this slow sinking into something like wet concrete rapidly drying and I must use my wits to get out of it while I can.

"I thought you said you don't practice that kind of medicine anymore," I say slowly.

Her grin fades and she lets the hair go. It flies away in the wind. "I don't."

"Anyway, I do not want your secrets. You claim I'm here to seek your secret for generating wealth. Did all your years of practicing witchcraft lead you to this?" I throw out my hand as if encircling her yard and house. "You have nothing to envy or desire. No treasure here. So why should I listen to you? What secrets do you have to share?"

She smiles, almost delighted with my words. "What is it you see when you look at my yard?"

Strange statues and animal parts. Things scattered randomly throughout. Old clothing piled in corners. Yet no matter that it is full, it feels *so much* empty.

"Rubbish," I say. "If I were to step into your yard, I would feel like I was suffocating." Madness—that is what I see in all those statues.

Complete and utter madness. And that is nothing I wish to step into. Oh, mysterious ancestors, please tell me why you sent me here.

"It is a problem, this thing you have of not seeing," she says. "A sangoma is only as powerful as her eyes. You think you see but you cannot see through the darkness. You see light only."

"Then how is it I see you? You are not light."

"That is what you think," she says, "because you see only what you expect to see. That is your weakness. Do you think there is no light in darkness? And no truth in evil?"

My lips feel dry. I have no response. Her words are like being knocked over by a goat.

"You crave order," she says, "you fear anything else and so you cannot help people in their chaos."

"No, you are lying!" I shout but I feel it, this deep fear filling up the emptiness inside of me. I thought I was full too, though not full of concrete statues and animal parts, full of good things like love for Zi and Little Man and now Sifiso and the people the amadlozi send to me but here it is: nothing. Nothing at all inside except fear.

I gulp back the sudden sob and a tear rolls down my cheek.

"Wena, you may lack eyes, but do you have ears? Listen! The ancestors sent you here."

"I know," I say, subdued.

"Your problem, little girl, is that you don't understand evil." There is something in her voice that inevitably becomes a cackle, no matter how serious she is being. "You don't even *want* to understand evil. How do you expect to fight evil if you do not understand it? If you cannot sympathize with it?"

"Sympathize with evil?" Everything in me wants to recoil, to reach back in my mind and deflect her words and her presence. And yet the amadlozi sent me here. That includes not just goat-woman but Gogo and Mkhulu. Maybe even Mama. Am I meant to learn from her or learn despite her? "I won't choose evil," I say. "I refuse."

She laughs at me. "Stupid child." As she laughs, head back, there's nothing to block the stench of her mouth.

Zi flinches and shrinks behind my back.

"Did you never read the Bible?" she asks. "*Be wise as serpents, innocent as doves.* You," she belches in my face. "You are a failure. Hah! You'll never be the sangoma you could be or that you want to be because you lack the fundamental, most important skill a sangoma possesses."

"What?" I ask. A little desperate. "What is it? What do I lack?"

"Hah! Hah hah hah! I just told you…and yet still *you don't know.* Go away. Hambani, both of you, get out of here before I show you what I'd like to do to you." She gets down on both knees and then her belly and slithers right through the holes of the gate and towards us, stinging Zi's legs with her mouth as Zi starts screaming. "I'm going to eat you, little girl," she hisses. "You're going to go down my belly in the dark…"

Nhlanhla nips at her. Half of her face splits open, revealing her rotting teeth, and she snarls at her.

Cha! No, she isn't getting away with this. I hold up my hand. "Leave Nhlanhla alone."

She dances and sways, imitating a cobra, growing taller and taller and taller until we're looking the serpent in the face.

"You want power?" she asks. "*You'll* never have power."

I reach out and grab her by the throat. "And I already said you are a liar," I say. "I will have power. I will be more powerful than you ever were. But I will use my power for good."

She's choking for a second, starts shrinking until I'm no longer looking at a serpent but only the old woman—an aging, ugly witch. She has the ability to look like anything she wants, to make herself appear beautiful, but I have to respect her for this at least: she doesn't lie about who she is.

I let go and she gags a little, gasping for air.

"Siyahamba, Zi," I say.

Taking Zi's hand and clicking my tongue at Nhlanhla to come, I turn around and march back down the hill.

"Don't be so afraid all the time," the witch calls after me. "If amadlozi brought you here, they are telling you not to fear all these many things."

My legs are wobbly and I squeeze Zi's hand hard.

What was that about, Mkhulu?

Didn't you listen to her? he says. If you were listening, she told you exactly what you need to know.

His voice shuts off in an annoyed, hopeless sort of huff and I realize that I'm alone. That's an awkward feeling. So much of the day and night, I spend navigating their voices, trying to please them. And then when they suddenly disappear? I wonder what I did wrong. Like just now. The witch said I was useless. And apparently, the witch handed me some nugget of wisdom and I didn't recognize it. I hope it's not gone forever.

CHAPTER TWENTY-EIGHT

The End of Everything

"Are we going home now, Khosi?" Zi asks in a small voice as we walk away from the witch's house. "Now now, not just now…"

"Angazi," I reply because I don't know. Mkhulu is silent. Gogo is silent. They are both angry with me because I didn't understand what they were trying to tell me through the witch.

I reach back in my mind seeking another ancestor, one of those who speaks less frequently but is still there. But they too feel distant, ever receding somewhere into the darkness. As if they are taunting me. *She said you only see the light so let's see if you find us lurking here in the murky half-light of beyond.*

"Why not?" Zi asks. "I just want to go home." She sounds on the verge of tears.

I sigh. "Ngiyazi," I say. "Let's go home." If the amadlozi tell me nothing, what else can they expect me to do? I shoulder our bags and the water I had brought, expecting a long journey, and we head back towards our house, a short fifteen-minute walk away.

Though still dark, it is nearing dawn now. People are already beginning to stir. Light spills out of windows as the men and women inside ready themselves for work and children prepare for school. In the spots without formal houses, where squatters have built some few houses, someone has lit a fire, and people gather round, warming their hands or boiling water for cooking. Roosters crow, pecking the ground, pecking the chickens that mill about them. A brown Hadeda with white and pink markings and a purple-black beak lets loose its honking morning cry as it takes off into the air. It lands in the road in front of us, strutting across the road, glancing at us as if to say, "Good morning, we are the best thing in all of Imbali."

Zi takes my hand. I notice how small her hand is, and how thin. It feels as though she is shrinking. As though she is disappearing.

I glance at her sideways. Zi, my little Zi. Always so full of spirit but what now? Is she disappearing because of things I am failing to give her? Adequate food, nutrition, spiritual and intellectual and emotional sustenance? Or is it her fate to shrivel up and go away and it would happen anyway, no matter what I did or did not do?

Cha, it can't be her fate.

Clutching her tiny fingers, I make a small promise to myself that things will be different moving forward. I don't know how but tomorrow is a new day. I can change things. I can seek something else. I can do something else though God knows what, given the fact that if I thwart myself from the path of the sangoma, the amadlozi will torment me. I will become ill in body and spirit. But surely there has to be a way to feed us better than this.

We are nearing home now. And as we round the corner to the top of the hill where the burnt out shell of the tuck shop rests like a skeleton in shadow, the half-light of dawn illuminating its burnt out interior, we look down the hill at our house and see something that makes us both stop and draw back.

Three figures crouch at the door of our house. One is peeking in the window, the other is bent at the door handle with a hatchet, the third holds a gun in his hand, pointed at our front door.

I clap one hand around Nhlanhla's mouth, afraid she will bark and reveal us.

Zi whimpers and I clap the other hand around her mouth. But it's too late. The three figures look up and one of them spots us. Shouts. All three of them run towards us as fast as their legs can carry them.

"Run, Zi!" I shout.

Her hand's still in mine. We turn and run down the hill, towards the shops, towards the main road and city. She's slowing me down already but it doesn't matter, I could never leave her behind.

But what about Nhlanhla?

"Nhlanhla," I shout, turning back.

She has stopped. She stands like a sentinel, stock still in the middle of the road, growling.

The man carrying a gun aims it straight at her throat.

"No," I shout. "Nhlanhla, woza!"

She whines gently in her throat, letting me know she hears me. Yet her whole body is still as she waits for the man in front of her to make his move.

"Nhlanhla," I shout.

He cocks the gun. It makes a short, sharp clicking sound.

And she leaps towards him, lips pulled back, snarling.

He shoots.

Nhlanhla's body twists mid-air, thuds as she drops to the ground.

The sound is sudden and quick and then the world is oddly silent except for the slow gurgle of blood gushing from her throat.

"Nhlanhla," Zi cries, and moves as though she is going to run back.

Nhlanhla whimpers.

"No!" I shout, wrestling Zi's body until she faces forward. "We have to keep on going."

We have to, even though I already know it's useless. Whoever they are, they will hunt us down until they find us.

The man wielding the ax lurches towards us while the other kneels down and aims his gun. Will he really shoot us in the back?

"Run," I hiss, pushing Zi towards the empty field. "Run to Little Man's house. His mom will help you." I hope that is true, I must believe that is true. I have nowhere else to send her.

I wait just long enough to see her heading up the hill and then I start running the other way. If it is me they want, surely they will leave her alone.

The sound of a gunshot startles me so badly, I leap in the air. It feels like something lifts me higher than I could possibly have jumped. The bullet hits the ground, dust and stones spraying out and stinging my legs.

"Stop, I will kill you," one of the men yells.

I think I would keep going, even if they shot me, except I look back to make sure that Zi is gone, safe, disappeared up the hill towards Little Man's house. Instead, a fourth man is running back towards us, carrying her, holding her around the waist with one hand, his other hand covering her mouth. She's kicking and flailing but he ignores her and marches towards the men hunting us.

I halt.

There is nothing that anybody could say or do that would convince me to leave Zi in danger, just to save myself.

"Zi, kulungile?" I shout.

"Ow!" It's the man gripping her who screams, suddenly, his hand dropping from her mouth. He punches her on the side of her head. She stops struggling and starts crying, loud sobbing noises you could hear a kilometer away. He claps his hand back over her mouth.

Slowly, I make my way back towards them.

"Please let her go," I say.

"She bit me," the man snarls. He yanks the braids on her head, hard. Her cry of pain is muffled by his hand.

"Just let her come and be beside me," I beg. "We won't resist. We will come with you. We will do whatever you want."

He lets her go and she runs to my side, burying her head in my side.

Mkhulu, if ever there was a time for you to protect me...to show up...a snake? A dragon? A dog? Anything?

But Mkhulu is silent.

Is he that angry with me for failing at the witch's house, that he would let me—and Zi—fall into harm's way?

Gogo?

Gogo, too, is silent.

Why won't you answer me, old ones? Please please please talk to me.

I'm the wayward child, the one nobody wants to show up at the birthday party. The one who burned all her bridges and has nobody to turn to when she needs help.

But I didn't burn any bridges. I just...didn't understand. So why won't you help me?

My eyes drift from Nhlanhla's body to the men, to the silent houses all around us.

Mkhulu said that doing the right thing does not mean you are protected from harm. I straighten my back. In all the thousands of years that humans have lived on this earth, people have suffered, many of them worse than I will. Some deserved what they got...but most did not.

I remember too the readings in church about Jesus' suffering leading up to his death on the cross, how even though he was God's son, he was bruised and broken and battered. And, I think now, if we claim he knew the full range of human experience, then he must have experienced literally everything—I mean everything, even the violation that women endure. He must know what it is like to lose everything. He must know what it is like to have nothing, to leave everything you know and love for some other place. The way Ahmed and his wife did. Is this my path too?

And then I think about the witch, how she told me I must sympathize with evil to understand it. What does that mean?

"What do you want from us?" I ask the men now surrounding us. I don't recognize them. I don't know who they are so I don't know why they are here. If I did, perhaps I could address them, answer some questions, convince them to let us go.

"Just come with us," the man with the ax says.

We walk down the street towards Nhlanhla. Her sides are still heaving softly, blood bubbling through her mouth. Zi sobs quietly beside me.

"May we have a second with her?" I ask.

The man with the ax hesitates.

"No," the man with the gun barks at us. "Just keep walking."

I stare at him. I stare until he grows uncomfortable. Then I say, quietly, so that he knows I mean it: "I will go with you but I need a minute to help my dog go to the ancestors."

He glances nervously at the other men until one of them finally growls, "Let her do it, Mdu. But hurry."

Zi and I kneel beside Nhlanhla. I lean in close, my lips near her ear. "Thank you, Nhlanhla," I whisper. "Thank you for giving up your life for us."

She lifts her tail in one last, final thump, and her chest slowly stills.

Take her, Mkhulu. Take her, Gogo. You sent her to us to watch over us. Thank you. Now take her to be with you and treat her well.

She's no longer breathing. Her body is still warm. I keep my hand on her side. I breathe in and out. Her spirit is leaving, slow-slow. Leaving. Leaving. And finally gone.

Mdu digs the gun sharply into my ribs. "Your dog's dead," he says. "Let's go. Asambeni!"

I take Zi's hand and help her to her feet. "Gogo will take care of her, Zi," I whisper.

Zi sniffles. "You promise?"

I squeeze her hand and we walk, the men around us on all sides, past our house, past MaDudu's house, towards a khumbi parked at the intersection of our road and the next. As we pass MaDudu's house, I hope for a minute that she will come outside and see us, so that she can call the police.

But no. No, Gogo, keep her safe and asleep, inside, because surely these men would shoot her to keep her silent if she came outside.

So we are quiet and nobody comes out, not from any house. No flutter of curtains at windows. No uncle stumbling inside after a long night drinking. No mama stirring early to cook breakfast, lights spilling out of an open kitchen door. In all of Imbali, in every neighborhood, people are getting ready for the day. But on our street, the houses are still dark.

And so, nobody sees them take us. Nobody sees when Mdu herds us into the khumbi.

As the door slams shut, it sounds like a punctuation mark, *full stop*, declaring the end. The end of everything I have ever known.

CHAPTER TWENTY-NINE

I'll Get Her Out of This, Mama

Zi huddles against me as the men pile in, two of them in the front, the others sitting right next to us, shoving us until the metal digs into my side. They slam the doors shut and start the engine.

Mdu eyes me, keeping his gun focused on Zi. He understands my weak spot. He knows what I can never let go of. Not even the amadlozi could make me. I would go crazy first.

I put my arm around her and stare at him.

"No matter what happens to me," I say deliberately, "you and your brothers have cursed yourselves."

His lip curls up. "Oh, are you a witch now? Are you calling down all your evil powers upon us?"

The driver glances back quickly. "Is she admitting it? That she's a witch?"

I laugh. "I don't have to be an umthakathi to understand what is going to happen to you." I point my chin at the man in the driver's seat. "He will die a violent death." I nod at the man in the passenger seat. "He will also die a violent death." And then I nod at Mdu. "And you? It'll be slow and painful. It'll take a long, long time. Years, in fact. You'll be betrayed by these very men you think are your friends and brothers."

He sneers at me but the driver jerks the car as though startled.

"Hey, watch it," Mdu yells. I think he's yelling at me.

We drive past Nhlanhla's body, a cold lump on the hard earth. We turn right and another right, then down the road and past the shops on our left to the main road towards town.

"Let me have your phone," Mdu says.

"You can't avoid the truth," I say.

"Shut up and give me your phone," he snarls.

I picture my phone at home, beside my bed. I didn't bring it because the amadlozi were sending me on a journey and I didn't know when we'd be returning. The last journey did not involve electricity. I was out in the wilderness for a month, in the snow, the rain, the wind…swimming through the river and down to the ocean… So this time, when they told me *go*, I didn't bother packing something that would only be a burden.

Am I still on the journey, Gogo? Or was it abandoned and this is a different plan? And would you please answer me?

I wish I had brought it. I could have texted or called Sifiso by now.

"I don't have a phone," I tell him. "It's at my house."

He glares at me, unbelieving.

I empty the pockets on my jacket and then my skirt. I open my bag and show him the jugs of water and Maric biscuits, but no phone. "See?"

"What about her?" he asks of Zi.

"If she has a cell phone, I don't even know about it," I say. "What about it, Zi? Do you have a cell phone?"

"If I had a cell phone, I would have already called Sifiso," she says. She turns to the men. "Do you know who Sifiso is?"

"Who?" the driver asks. "Sifiso who? I don't know this Sifiso."

I nudge Zi and shake my head at her. The last thing they need is to hear her say, "He's a policeman and he's in love with my sister." We don't know who these men are or why they've taken us but the less they know, the better for us. We need to keep them distracted. Zi opens her backpack and shows Mdu the loaf of bread and oranges I packed inside. Mdu slings our bags into the back of the khumbi and slumps against the seat, glaring at us.

"What do you want from us?" I ask again.

One of them grunts. That is the only answer it seems they will give me.

I look out the window. Zi shrugs into me and I put an arm around her and kiss her curly hair. I'll get her out of this, Mama, I promise.

Even as the words roll through my head, I stop short, realizing this is the first time I've ever addressed Mama as one of the ancestors.

CHAPTER THIRTY

THE LIZARD WAS WRONG

The road from Imbali to Pietermaritzburg is short and the landscape barren and ugly. Trash is strewn on all sides of the street and up against fences and walls. On either side of the road, factory buildings, petrol stations, and shacks burrow close to the ground. We approach the city and move towards the city center. At one time, I imagine this was a beautiful place, with its stately red-brick buildings, the museum with Grecian columns, the statue of Gandhi, the classic style building with a lion and unicorn etched in stone. All very European but now the African parts creep in, with the people and the bustle and the noise and the...well, all the people. We crowd in here and we make it ours. It's not always lovely, not in that empty grandiose museum building kind of way, but it's beautiful in its own way. It's ours. It's us. We make it beautiful because we are beautiful.

I look at the men who have captured us and I realize that they, too, are beautiful in their own way. They have beautiful black skin and white teeth and big noses and strong arms. They stare out the windows, their jaws set and their profiles something worthy of statues.

And I realize that even if I don't know why they've kidnapped us, and no matter what happens, I can recognize that even a little bit of the spirit or soul within them each is good and worthy of love.

We pull into the Scottsville shopping mall, and the man closest to us hands me two blue cloths and motions for me to tie blindfolds, first around Zi and then around myself. I tie a cloth around Zi, trying to leave gaps so she can see. Her breathing gets fast and she grips my hand and I whisper, "I'm right here. You won't be able to see but I'm right here." I leave what I think is a subtle gap in my own blindfold but he reaches forward and adjusts it so that all I can see is blue.

"Hamba, hamba," he yells at the driver, and we're off.

Mdu leans closer and whispers, "I'm keeping the gun aimed at your sister. Can you do anything about that, umthakathi?"

"I'm not a witch," I mumble.

He snickers.

I follow the direction for the first few turns but the driver is going fast fast and swerving around corners. Then at some point, he must get onto the N3, because we're speeding along without any stops. But I can't tell if we're headed towards Durban or the opposite way, towards Howick, because we took so many twists and turns before we exited town.

Who are these men and what do they want with me? With us?

If I had a better idea who was behind this, Gogo, I'd know how much danger we are in. Just a little bit or a whole lot.

I don't need to know the name of my enemy to know the danger we are in. But to solve this thing, I must know, Who is my enemy? My mind races through the possibilities.

Little Man is mixed up in some terrible things. And Langa knew that he was my boyfriend. Could this be Langa and his men? But why would I be a threat to the taxi wars? Unless, as they say, they really believe I'm a witch and somehow on Little Man and Bo's side.

Or perhaps it is Bo, believing I am a threat to Little Man and to his attempt to take over a taxi route

But then I have to think about what happened with Ahmed, too. That was surely a warning, that they killed him and left his body at my gate. Was that related to the taxi wars? Or was that related to MaNene and her terrible sons? Am I a threat to those who would expel the outsiders from Imbali?

Who has sent these men to harm us—Langa, Bo, or the Nenes?

Perhaps there is something else, something I am missing. My head aches as I try to recall something that would show me what I need to know.

I start to get hot and thirsty. The blue cloth bites into my skin.

"Kulungile, Zi?" I ask.

She doesn't answer but she presses hard against me.

My bladder starts to ache. The baby nestled into the folds of my stomach, pressing against it.

It's hard to imagine comfort. Or home. They are taking us so far away…it's hard to imagine that I'll ever be able to return. The longer we drive, the more impossible our situation seems.

The khumbi slows and begins to swerve, this way and that. We must have exited the N3. We are going up, so perhaps we are heading towards Hillcrest and the Valley of a Thousand Hills. But we could have gone a different direction, towards the Drakensburg Mountains instead. I'm really lost. It's impossible to tell which direction we took, only that we are headed up.

"What is it you want with us? Who are you taking us to? Or where?"

"Shut up," Mdu growls.

"If she really is a witch, don't you think she would know?" one of the other men asks—the driver, from the direction of the voice.

At that moment, my stomach erupts in tiny little flutters, a million little wings beating against my rib cage. Along with it, joy and hope. Oh, little baby. You're in there. You're in there and you're alive.

"I need to use the toilet," Zi whispers.

We could make a run for it, if we had just that much space and just that much time to do it.

"Can you please let us go to the toilet?" I ask.

The driver starts cursing in Zulu. "You better not pee all over my car, Ntombi," he yells.

A small part of me is terribly afraid of these men and what they might do. Another part realizes—no matter what happens, it is not the end, it is just the next thing. The Lizard was wrong, the Chameleon was right. We will join the herd—the millions of amadlozi on the other side, like the millions of zebra and wildebeest and springbok that moved across the land in the days before Europeans came to Africa.

So I am not afraid, not for me. But Zi is just nine. And this unborn baby, not much more than a peanut inside me but alive with possibility. For Zi, for my baby, I will fight. And for Sifiso, because I do care. I will fight for Sifiso, whether I ever see him again or not. Even for Little Man, even if he is no longer mine to fight for.

It's not time to die yet. At least, not willingly.

"If you don't let us go to the toilet, we're both going to pee all over your car," I say. "And Mdu, we are sitting on the same seat so you will sit in our urine too."

"Pull over, Lethabo," Mdu shouts. "Pull over now."

The khumbi swerves off the road and slams to a stop. I hear the door sliding open. Mdu shoves me from behind, he's in such a hurry to get us out of the car.

"Can we please take our blindfolds off?" I ask. "I don't know how we can go without that."

"Yes, but if you do anything stupid, Ntombi—" He makes a click click sound with his tongue and then he pulls back the trigger of the gun so we hear the real click sound.

Zi jumps and recoils, leaning into me.

"Shhh," I whisper, removing my blindfold and then Zi's, and looking around to see where we are.

It looks like an informal settlement in the veld, the houses built of tin sheets or gathered sticks, multi-colored cloths draped here and there to keep wind from whistling between cracks and holes. Smoke rises from campfires and a goat bleats loudly.

Something in the sunlight beyond the shacks. My stomach cramps in sudden excitement, and I squint to see further. Yes, in the distance, about half a kilometer away—it's a reservoir of some kind. Swollen from the October rains.

Water.

Mdu prods me. "Let's go let's go let's go!" He sounds just like a khumbi driver, or the one who takes the fares. I've heard Little Man shouting the same thing, hitting the side of the van as they careen away to get more passengers at the next stop. "Let's go let's go let's go!"

And suddenly, all at once, as if they have broken their embargo on words, the amadlozi shout the same thing in my head. Now now now, they scream. Hamba hamba hamba. Go go go!

"We're going to go behind that bush," I say, careful not to betray anything with my voice. But I hear it shaking just that little bit. Please Gogo, don't let them notice.

And he doesn't. Too impatient. "Hurry hurry," Mdu shouts.

"And don't try anything or we will shoot you," Lethabo yells.

I pull Zi in front of me, to protect her, and we head behind the bush.

"Zi," I hiss, "if you have to go, you can pee in your pants. We aren't taking the time to pee right now. As soon as I say go, you're running. Run as fast as you can go and don't stop, no matter what they do. We're heading for that water. As soon as we get there, I want you to jump in."

"I can't swim, Khosi," she whispers. Pleads. The begging in her voice.

Fear is a hyena, it slinks in, a coward. I will have to drop her in the water.

"Don't worry," I say. "I have a plan."

"But I can't swim," she says again, more urgent this time.

"Shut up," I hiss.

We duck around the bush. I tug Zi's hand and begin to run and she has no choice now, she has to follow.

We run. I try to keep us in a straight line behind the bush and out of the line of their sight as long as possible. But it is just some few seconds and Mdu shouts, "Hawu!"

The khumbi revs, tires squealing as Lethabo spins around, and drives off road. Bits of dirt and rocks spray upward from the tires as it rumbles towards us. The door swings open. Mdu appears at the door, ready to jump out and start chase or perhaps just nab us and drag us inside.

A hollow to the right looks like it could stop them.

"Turn right, Zi," I shout, and push her towards it.

The khumbi swerves, tries to stop as Lethabo sees the ditch. Too late. They pitch headfirst into the ditch and stall.

"Hamba hamba," I yell at Zi.

Already Mdu has leapt from the khumbi. He stumbles after us. Scrambles over the ground we've covered, waving his gun in the air.

Turn left, Mkhulu says.

"Left, Zi, left," I hiss, and we jerk left, following a small path that crumbles as it inclines down towards the water.

The men's shouts recede to a dim roar as we run. I'm concentrating too hard on getting there, I can't pay attention to what what what they're yelling. I look behind us. Once, and then once again.

Mdu stops. He aims the gun.

And then all at once the witch blocks the path. She's waiting, a lion tail in her hand. She lifts her hands to the sky and the lion's tail switches back and forth.

I stop, unsure. Is Zi safer behind me, where Mdu is shooting at us, or in front, where the witch could take her? I jerk Zi behind me, then again in front of me, then behind again. What should I do, Mkhulu? What should I do? Oh, Mama, please. What should I do?

Zi stumbles. I jerk her up.

"What's going on?" she gasps.

And I realize she can't see the woman who wanted to take her, who offered me money for her.

"Leave us alone," I scream at the witch.

She cackles. "You can't even see help when it's right in front of you," she shouts. "Didn't the amadlozi send you to me so I could teach you?"

She swats the lion's tail towards me. It whips up little dust devils with its hard flicking motion. She may be old but she's still strong, her arm muscles sinewy and bulging from her skinny arms as she flogs the dirt.

Despite her words, she is a threat.

Our eyes meet. Hers, gold-flecked, like her gold tooth, symbolic of her lifetime in pursuit of wealth only, no matter the consequence to others.

And I remember Mama. How Mama was all good, all good, so good that it was hard to believe she could do this thing, steal money from our neighbor. But she did.

And I think of Auntie Phumzi, who has always been a strong Christian

Zionist, one of those who believes there is right and there is wrong, and she must choose the right side. Yet she is the one who has decided I am a witch and so she has turned her back on her own family, its own kind of evil.

And here is umthakathi, right in front of me. She is thoroughly evil, and how can I, even for a minute, think that she could be offering her help? It is impossible.

"They are telling you to go," she says now. "They are telling you to trust. You grasp so hard that you cannot hear. Go. Go now."

And she's right. The amadlozi are indeed saying that, and the one ancestor, she is speaking to both of us. I cannot believe I have an ancestor in common with this enemy in front of me. But I do.

I shudder over the side of the path, a steep hill straight to the water's edge, and Zi follows just behind me. A bullet zings past. Dirt and pebbles sting my legs as we slide down the slope, straight towards the water.

In front of us again, the witch is juddering over boulders. She leaps from one to another without pausing. She lifts her hand with the lion's tail. Lightning crackles across the sky and hits the water, light rippling across its surface.

We're at the water's edge now.

What should I do? If we jump in the water, will we die from the lightning bolts shooting electricity in the water?

"Hamba," the umthakathi shouts. "Jump in the water."

Hamba, Mkhulu commands. Jump in the water.

Mdu halts. "Come back," he yells. "Or I'll kill you."

Zi holds back, yanking my hand as if to say, Wait. Wait.

But I can't wait anymore. Here is the water, my gift and perhaps even my curse. Sometimes we don't realize how something can be both.

I don't wait for Zi to assent, I grab her hand and pull her in. To the right, a bullet pings the water. To the left, the witch watches with slit eyes, the lion's tail whipping around in her hand. I look at her and nod. She nods back, we're allies now, and she turns around to face Mdu.

Zi's eyes are huge and she's squeezing my hand so hard, it's bound to be misshapen from now on, her grip is that tight, but I put my other hand to her lips to stop the panicky words burbling from her lips.

Like all Catholics, I was a baby when I was baptized. I don't remember when the priest doused me with holy water, claiming me for God. But I do remember Zi's baptism: her puckered lips, the way she squalled as water hit her face, the priest laughing and handing her back to Mama, Mama's solemn face and the twinkle in Baba's eye. Gogo and I stood behind them, Gogo's hand on my back.

Water. It's life, and it's death, and it's…everything.

Zi's sobs are the only thing I hear as I grab her around the waist and pull her under water.

CHAPTER THIRTY-ONE

My Own Threat

The water is cold and clear.

Zi's eyes are closed, her mouth opened in a silent scream.

There's no time to stop. I swim, drag her alongside me, kick to go deeper. Where the water is murky. Where fish skim the mud bottoms. Where these men can't follow. The witch could follow but she won't. She isn't a threat, at least, she's no longer a threat, for some few minutes. Perhaps my own worst threat has been myself. My own unwillingness to see what the amadlozi were trying to tell me.

These men will assume we have drowned. Perhaps they will wait to see if my body surfaces, or Zi's. But they won't wait long. We need to stay submerged, to keep swimming until we find the downstream current.

I've been here before and my body recognizes it. The Umgeni River. This feels like home. It is here where I learned my power, so long ago.

The reservoir is created by a dam and I need to find the outlet. So I swim where the voices tell me to go. Looking back, I see that Zi's eyes are screwed shut, tight tight, but she is no longer panicking.

I swim, dragging Zi behind me, until we reach a current. It pulls us in a southeastern direction. Exactly where we want to go.

I let go.

Our bodies tumble in the current and it pulls us toward the mouth of the river. Toward the Indian Ocean.

I let my thoughts tumble too. Let them go where they will, the water taking our bodies and my thoughts towards the vastness of the sea.

Even in the cold water, my eyes are hot with tears.

I wanted to leave and the amadlozi told me no no no, don't leave. And now I can't go back. Because of Little Man. Langa. Bo. Gladys Nene. And Auntie Phumzile.

Oh, yes, Auntie Phumzi. The one who believes I'm a witch, and that I killed Gogo.

What was it the amadlozi told me? Open your eyes. Open—open—open your eyes!

The enemy has become an ally; my family—the enemy.

Because of the past month's rains, the river is high. In places, it is so deep, we drift along like bottom feeders, keeping ourselves invisible from passers-by. But still, there are shallow spots where we stand up and walk, water and mud dripping down our legs.

"Do we have to keep swimming?" Zi groans. "Can't we find a road and somebody will pick us up to give us a ride?"

"Hawu, do you want to get robbed and beaten?" I ask.

"What would they take? Do you have any money that they could steal from us?"

I ignore her question. She's too little to know what they might try to take. "We are going to keep going all the way to the ocean," I say.

"What about a taxi? Do we have money to catch a taxi?"

I actually do have some few rands stashed in a pocket. I pat it in sudden panic to make sure it's still there.

"Zi, whatever money I have, we are going to need it, I promise you. We must just keep swimming."

"Ugh," she groans.

"Listen," I say, "I'm doing all the hard work. And besides, you never knew you could breathe under water, did you?"

"Khosi." Zi shakes her head at me. "I still can't breathe under water. I don't know what's happening, but I know it's impossible to breathe under water."

"The amadlozi can do anything," I say. "Just don't ask me what our plan is when we reach the ocean, Zi. Because I don't know. I only know we can't go back."

Big fat tears roll down Zi's cheeks. They spark a response in my own. My eyes feel raw and red, from the water and from crying while we drifted down the river.

"What about Sifiso?" she asks.

I shake my head. I wish I knew.

"What about Little Man?"

"Zi, we must keep going."

We've reached another deep spot, water up to our waists and about to get deeper. I ignore her tears. I have to. "Come," I say, and push her under.

The river wends its way through the country. Thick bushes grow just past the riverbanks, and occasional huts or businesses pop into view. We stay under water as much as possible but occasionally, we surface, when it isn't deep enough. Thankfully, we don't encounter another human, though we see the smoke from cook fires rising just past the first layer of bushes and on one riverbank, clothes spread out to dry from some woman's washing.

Finally, we reach the city. Durban. Houses and businesses are closer to the riverbanks now, and for awhile, it runs right next to a busy street. We submerge to pass under the overpasses and bridges, until the river widens at its mouth and rushes towards the sea.

Soaked, muddy, bone-tired, we crawl out of the water at the ocean's edge, where fresh water and salt water mix.

I put a finger in my mouth and taste the salt.

CHAPTER THIRTY-TWO

My Ocean

A family is picnicking on the beach, parents and their three children. They look startled when Zi and I appear in our mud-drenched clothes. The mother gives a little half-scream and then stops herself. "Shame," she says. "Are you girls all-right? Must we call the police?"

"No, Mama, it's OK. But may we use your cell phone?" I pull a ten-rand note from my pocket. It is soaking wet, like me.

"I don't need your money," the woman says. She looks at her husband and he nods. She hands me her cell phone.

I dial his number. Yes, it is burned into my memory.

"Hello?"

I want to cry when I hear his voice, full of warmth. He is a safe place. I wish I could just crawl into his safety.

"Hello?" he repeats. "Who is it?"

"Sifiso," I say. "It's Khosi." My lips feel numb. Perhaps from the cold. Perhaps a little bit from fear.

"Khosi," Sifiso shouts. There are tears of joy in his voice. "Oh, thank God. I have been calling and calling you. Are you safe?"

So news of our abduction must have gotten out after all. "Yes, I am safe. Did you hear already? Did somebody see?"

But he's babbling. "I was so afraid the two of you were caught inside. I was so afraid you were dead. Is Zi with you? Is she safe?"

He's not making any sense. "What do you mean?" I ask.

"I'm here at your house. There's a fire. Your house—it's burnt to the ground. It's ashes."

"What?" I still don't understand. We were just there, and now the house is gone?

"We were so worried, Khosi," he says. "It was burning too hot for us to go inside to find you and Zi. It looks as though somebody doused the house in petrol. I'm sorry, Khosi, your hut has burned down too. Completely. There is nothing left."

"Why? Who—?"

"Where are you?" His voice drops low. "I need to see you. I need to touch you. It is the only way—Khosi. I need to know you are all right."

My heart feels like it's flying through my mouth and it's beating beating. I want to see him too. But—

"I'm all right, really," I say. "I'm all right."

He lets out a long, slow breath. "When will I see you?"

"Angaz'," I say. "I am not in Imbali."

"We have questions for you. The police. Nhlanhla? She was shot dead? We found her in the street. What happened?"

"I have questions also," I say. And then I stop. This is not the time for questions. I already know who, what, why. The answer is "everybody" and "nobody." It doesn't matter whether this was my family, or the community, or the taxi drivers. No matter what the question is, the answer is: I can't go back.

The house is gone. I loved that house because it was the only house I knew. But now that Mama is gone, and Gogo is gone, and now that Auntie Phumzi came and took all of their things—it's a shell, empty of any reason to stay.

I already knew, but now I know even more. The amadlozi sent me on a journey and now they are making sure I don't go back. It is the gift of God, that we all receive blessings, even if we don't deserve it, or recognize them when they come.

We have nothing with us, it is true. OK, I have exactly ten rand in my pocket. Enough to buy a packet of Rooibos.

Yes, Mkhulu says. It is time.

Was this what it felt like, to be Ahmed and his wife when they left Somalia and came to South Africa? They had nothing, but they had each other.

"I am safe, Sifiso," I say at last. "But I am not coming back to Imbali."

Voice shaking, he asks, "What do you mean? Have you decided? About us, I mean? Is it no?"

"I don't know," I say. "But I will call you when I am settled. It may be some time…but I promise. I promise I will call. You can depend on that."

He is silent for a long while. Then: "Ngiyezwa." That is all. He understands. And I believe he does. Perhaps there is a future for us, down the way. Perhaps. If my will can make a way, it will happen. Durban is not so far from Pietermaritzburg. He could live here and work there. Or transfer. But first I must make a way for me and Zi to survive. To thrive. And I must have this baby and see how I am as a mother. I hope I am kind and funny and patient, like my own Mama was. And these are things I must do on my own, for a time, before I lean on somebody else.

"My aunt's name is Phumzile," I say. "Phumzile Zulu. She lives the other side of Imbali, near your mother. You should see what she knows about this fire. She accused me of witchcraft when Gogo died, because Gogo left me the house. She does not want me to have the house and now she has her wish."

"I will do that," he promises.

"Langa is in Edendale hospital," I say. "So is Little Man, my—my ex-boyfriend. I don't suppose you'll completely solve the taxi war by finding them…but it may help."

I remember the images I saw when I first listened to MaNene's ancestors. Two lions chasing after a gazelle. The gazelle's body, broken and mangled, lying in the dirt. A pool of blood mixing with earth.

I take a deep breath. Again, I am making guesses but I have no reason not to share these hunches with this man who loves me. Even if I don't deserve his love.

"And there is a woman named Gladys Nene," I say. "Find her. She lives in Imbali J somewhere, though I don't know where. She has two sons. Ask them about Ahmed, the Somali who owned the tuck shop, the one who was found dead against my gate. It is possible they were behind it. Or know who was behind it."

"Ngiyabonga," he says.

I suppose I could call Little Man but I already know that is a dead-end path. Someday I must tell him about the child but that can wait. He is too much caught up in this taxi war.

Instead, I hand the cell phone back to the kind lady who lent it to me and turn back to the parking lot and Zi. She is twirling in circles, making herself dizzy. Her hands are lifted to the sky. She staggers and almost falls, catches herself, looks toward me and grins. Then she starts twirling again.

I have no money. I have no job. I have no family. Except Zi. And, of course, the ancestors. I will always have them. Nor can I forget, I also have this baby, and she—yes, I already know, this baby is a she—she will ensure that when I die, I too am one of the ancestors.

We left everything behind and now it is all gone. Even Nhlanhla is gone. But we have each other and we have our lives. And we are here, at the ocean, my source. The place of my baptism into the life of a sangoma. And now, the beginning of my new life.

The ocean stretches out behind us, a vast roiling blue-grey soup of nothingness and...and everythingness.

I will name her Amanzi. Water. Because no matter where I go, I will have water. And here in Durban, I have an abundance of water, my power.

It's time, Mkhulu says, and it feels like I can hear Gogo's and Mama's emphatic nods.

The world is my ocean. I will find my way in it.

AUTHOR'S NOTE

It's a big responsibility to write a book set in a culture that is not your own. It is not a responsibility I take lightly. For many years, I have been lucky enough to be welcomed into South African homes from a diverse range of local cultures as a granddaughter, daughter, sister, auntie, and good friend. For all the many people I can't possibly name here who are friends and family, thank you from the bottom of my heart. Ngiyabonga kakhulu. Baie dankie fir alles. Obrigada. And—gracias.

I want to specifically thank my dear friends Futhi Ntshingila, Gugu Mafokeng, and Bukhosi Dube. The three of you helped this text reach a higher level of authenticity and accuracy and I can't thank you enough. I wish I lived close enough to see you all regularly but I will take the stolen moments we have and cherish them. And to Izak de Vries, friend and collaborator and colleague extraordinaire—thank you for the photo that graces the cover of this book, as well as your photo for *This Thing Called the Future*.

My brother Dumisani Dube died suddenly last year in South Africa at the age of 56. I will miss him always. This book is dedicated to him.

With lots of love to him and to all South Africans, everywhere!

CHARACTERS

Ahmed: the Somali tuck-shop owner in Khosi's neighborhood

Babaomkhulu / Mkhulu: Khosi's great-grandfather, now dead and one of the amadlozi

Beauty: Khosi's cousin, Phumzile's child

Bo: Little Man's boss, attempting to take over some of Langa's taxi routes

Elizabeth / Mama: Khosi's mother, dead for 3 years

Gladys Nene: one of Khosi's patients, a woman who seeks absolution for her sons' wrong-doings

Gogo: Khosi's grandmother, now dead and one of the amadlozi

Gogo / MaDudu: Khosi's next-door neighbor

Langa: taxi owner, a "big man" in Imbali

Lethabo: one of the thugs hired to kidnap Khosi and Zi; he's the driver

Little Man: Khosi's boyfriend

Liyana: (female Zulu name, means "It is raining") a toddler that Khosi heals

Lungile: Khosi's uncle, her mother's brother

"Makhosi": the sangoma who trained Khosi

Mdu: one of the thugs hired to kidnap Khosi and Zi

Nobuhle: Liyana's mother

Phumzile / Phumzi: Khosi's aunt, her mother's sister

Sifiso: police officer and love interest

Thandi: granddaughter to "Makhosi," formerly Khosi's best friend

Zi/Zinhle: Khosi's little sister

GLOSSARY

Amadlozi: the ancestors.

Amadube: zebras.

AmaShembe: a distinctly African religious group that emerged originally from mission Christianity but combines elements of Christianity with Judaism, Scottish fashion, African culture, and African healing arts and mysticism.

Amasi: sour milk.

Amanzi: water.

Angaz'/Angazi: I don't know.

Asambeni: Let's go! (plural)

As-salaam 'alaikum: Peace be upon you. A greeting in Arabic.

Babomkhulu: grandfather.

Bakkie: a pickup truck

Bhuti: brother.

Blue spirit: a flammable liquid used in rituals by most traditional healers.

Braai: barbecue in Afrikaans.

Cha: No.

Emsamo: the part of a traditional hut where the amadlozi sit.

Futhi: again.

Gogo: grandmother.

Hamba / Hambani: Go! Run! Adding *ni* to the end makes the word plural.

Haibo: Wow!

Hawu: Wow!

Hheyi: Hey!

Ikhekhe: cake.

Imbali: flower, but also the name of a township outside of Pietermaritzburg, South Africa.

Impepho: incense or sage.

Inshallah: God willing. Arabic.

Inyama: meat.

Ja: yes or yeah in Afrikaans.

Khumbi: an African taxi.

Kodwa: but.

Kulungile: It's all-right. Or, as a question, Is everything all-right?

Kwenzenjani: What is it, or What is wrong?

Makhosi: an honorific title for sangomas.

Makoti: daughter-in-law.

Mealies: corn

Mfowethu: brother.

Mtanami: my child.

Muthi: medicine.

Ndodakazi: my daughter

Nee: no in Afrikaans

Ngeke: never

Ngikhathele: I'm tired.

Ngiyagula: I'm sick.

Ngiyakuthanda: I love you.

Ngiyabonga/Siyabonga: Thank you/We thank you.

Ngiyaqonda: I understand.

Ngiyezwa: I get it or I hear you.

Ngiyathembisa: I promise you.

Ngiyazi: I know.

Nina ninjani: How are you?

Nkulunkulu: God (literally "the old old one").

(i)Ntombi: girl.

(i)Ndodakazi: daughter.

(i)Ntombazane: little girl.

Phansi: down.

Phuthu: a corn porridge that the Zulus eat with meat and vegetables and gravy

Sala kahle: Stay well.

Sho: Sure! Said when someone is in agreement.

S'thandwa: an endearment like honey, sweetheart, lover.

Sangoma: a traditional Zulu healer.

Sawubona, Ahmed, nina ninjani: Hello, Ahmed, how are you and your family?

Shibhoshi: Jeyes Fluid

Sikhona: the response to "Nina ninjani" in Zulu greetings. It means "We are here" (literally), that is, "My family and I are well."

Siyahamba: We are going.

Spaza shop: a small convenience shop often run out of person's home. Stocks household items like soap or convenience store items like cigarettes and soda.

Thando: love.

Thwasa: an initiate, a person who is in the process of becoming a sangoma

Thula: shut up

Tokoloshe: a mythical creature in Zulu lexicon, a small hairy man that creates mischief

Toyi-toyi: a southern African dance that symbolizes the spirit of revolution and shaking off the shackles of oppression

Tsotsi: gangster

Ukugeza: cleansing.

Umthakathi: witch.

Utshwala: traditional Zulu beer.

Vuvuzela: a plastic horn that produces a loud monotone note.

Woza: come.

Wena: you.

Yebo: yes.

QUESTIONS FOR DISCUSSION

1. What similarities exist between your community and the community of Imbali? What differences? Do similarities outweigh the differences or vice versa?

2. South Africa is a multicultural society. What are some of the other cultures Khosi encounters or that are mentioned in *Under Water*? What are the benefits of living in a multicultural society? What problems can occur?

3. What personal challenges does Khosi face in this book? What political challenges does she face? How does she respond to irrational prejudice and accusations that she encounters, either directed towards herself or towards others?

4. Why is violence such a common feature of Khosi's life in Imbali township? What are Khosi's reflections--both private and verbalized--on the problem of violence?

5. Khosi's boyfriend Little Man gets sucked into the taxi war that begins to dominate life in Imbali. What are the causes of the taxi war? What are the consequences of the taxi war?

6. Khosi is a sangoma--a traditional healer in the Zulu tradition, which includes herbal remedies and communication with a host of ancestral spirits who help determine the source of patients' health issues. What are some of

the reasons patients come to visit Khosi? What are some differences and similarities between their understanding of illness and their definition of health issues and yours? Do you think medical doctors would be able to address the illnesses of Khosi's patients? Why or why not?

7. Khosi keeps very quiet about her pregnancy until her neighbor MaDudu confronts her with it. Why is Khosi so quiet about it? Are those the same reasons a seventeen-year-old American teenager would keep quiet about an unplanned pregnancy? Why or why not? What new challenges will Khosi face after her baby is born?

8. In many ways, Khosi must face the challenges of her life alone. What gives her strength? In other ways, Khosi is not alone. Who is on her side and how do they offer Khosi support?

9. Khosi struggles to reconcile the spiritual differences between her Catholic faith and her relationship with her ancestors. What are the tensions between the two? Does Khosi ever find a balance or an answer? Why or why not? Will this continue to be a struggle for her going forward? Why or why not?

10. Khosi talks about water as the source of her healing power. How does Khosi use water in her healing practice? What does water symbolize in this book?